ANGEL IN DISGUISE

Neurosurgeon Tom Galvan is one of the most brilliant men at St Joseph's Hospital. When he is seriously injured in a car crash, everyone is stunned — could this be the end of his career? No one is more anxious than Staff Nurse Christie Wisdom, who has the job of nursing him through it — and who is dismayed to find that the nurse-patient relationship develops into something far warmer, on her part at any rate . . .

Books by Anna Ramsay
in the Linford Romance Library:

MISTLETOE MEDICINE
HEARTBEAT
SURGEON IN PORTUGAL
CINDERELLA SRN
ACCIDENT PRONE

ANNA RAMSAY

ANGEL IN DISGUISE

Complete and Unabridged

LINFORD
Leicester

First published in Great Britain in 1987

First Linford Edition
published 2014

A catalogue record for this book is available
from the British Library.

ISBN 978–1–4448–1974–8

Published by
F. A. Thorpe (Publishing)
Anstey, Leicestershire

Set by Words & Graphics Ltd.
Anstey, Leicestershire
Printed and bound in Great Britain by
T. J. International Ltd., Padstow, Cornwall

This book is printed on acid-free paper

1

The air was mild for an April evening and Staff Nurse Wisdom had taken off her navy reefer jacket. She swung the black Metro expertly into the car park and reversed into a space, switched off the engine and sat for a moment, her high smooth brow a trifle creased in thought. 'Did I remember to leave a light on in the cottage? Am I *certain* I locked that back door?'

She'd spent the afternoon in her patchwork garden splitting clumps of snowdrops and purple-and-gold crocus, and planting out the Little Gem lettuces started from seed on the kitchen windowsill. Her hands felt even rougher than usual after being scrubbed with a nailbrush. But Christie Wisdom was considerate of her patients' comfort; she always carried a small tin of handcream in the pocket of her uniform.

Living alone, Christie had acquired the habit of talking to herself. 'What a long dreary winter this has been — but fingers crossed, we're into spring weather now. No more weekends like the last one,' she shivered involuntarily, 'black ice on the motorway and drivers behaving like maniacs in spite of police warnings.'

St Joseph's, having the nearest and most convenient Accident and Emergency Department, was used to coping with the grisly aftermath of road tragedies. Christie Wisdom had been one of the exhausted team of doctors and nurses struggling through a night they might prefer to forget but could not.

Delving inside the glove compartment, she retrieved a flimsy blue aerogramme and slid lithely from the driver's seat. This wouldn't take a couple of minutes. Nip out of the hospital gates and across the main road to the pillarbox, then dodging the beams of headlights dash back to Matilda the Metro to hook the Krooklok between steering wheel and clutch pedal and collect jacket and bag from the rear seat.

Each week on the same day, Thursday, Christie wrote to her mother, remarried and living in Zurich. News was always much the same — improvements made to the cottage, routine maintenance of Matilda, nursing exams passed, and incidents in the professional life of Christie Wisdom, newly qualified Registered General Nurse at St Joseph's Hospital in the heart of Wessex.

Mention, of course, of her boy-friend of the past fifteen months — Dr James Mallory, pathologist, thirty next birthday, six years older than Christie herself.

Not that there was anything exciting to relate where the sober and sensible James was concerned. Excitement was not his business, not what James was all about. Or Christie either. She and

James were very similar, both of them intent on leading *useful* lives, absorbed in their work and grateful for being able to slot into secure niches in their professions.

And, for Christie, something else: an urgent sense of wanting to be needed by the men and women and children she helped nurse back to health and strength; depended upon by those for whom she cared, her patients.

No one had ever needed her much before . . . Until the one time when she had been powerless to help.

★ ★ ★

Christie Wisdom was not a flippant sort of girl. She was, after all, twenty-four years old and had entered nursing at a later age than most young women. And for a very serious reason, which perhaps only her mother entirely understood.

Concealed by the darkness, a man was watching Christie as unawares she tucked her bag under her arm, slung her jacket over her shoulder and made her way across the half-empty staff car park.

Her body could never *unlearn* the rigorous training of Lucie Clayton's school of modelling — even if it had been six years ago. And it was Nurse Wisdom's distinctive walk which mesmerised the watcher's eye. Outlined in narrow black velvet jeans, the long elegant legs swung confidently loose-limbed from the hip, baggy dark sweater shrouding the girl from throat to thigh, the waterfall-straight brown hair falling smoothly from a high forehead to swing below narrow shoulderblades. Pale oval face calm and apparently expressionless in the lamplight as she headed for the lights of Casualty.

'Goodnight, Mr Galvan,' she acknowledged courteously as she passed the neurosurgeon, Tom Galvan, grinding out a cigarette stub on the tarmac beside his scarlet Porsche 924. Christie had noticed that one before, thought it a beauty

— and had wondered which lucky guy owned it. She was knowledgeable about cars. Dad . . . in his time he'd owned some real breathtakers.

But Christie's professional eye was critical as it took in the brooding hulk of Tom Galvan. There were more sensible ways of coping with the stresses of brain surgery than resorting to tobacco — but perhaps Mr Galvan lacked the self-control to give up smoking . . . *that* could never be said of James, so quiet and reliable and resolute.

Poor man, he looks weary, though, thought Christie, a sidelong glance showing her Mr Galvan's handsome features deeply lined and sallow in the lamplight.

Had she not recognised him she might even have been frightened. For his tall figure cast a forbidding shadow — heavy black overcoat collar pulled up to ruffle the curly hair at the nape of his neck, fumbling in his pockets for an elusive set of car keys. Exhaling cigarette smoke — she could smell it as she walked past — on to the exhilarating April night air.

'Goodnight.'

Tom frowned in conjecture.

He couldn't recall seeing her about the place before, but that purposeful sense of direction informed him that the girl with the mermaid hair worked at St Joseph's and must be coming on night duty. All the nurses generally seemed to know who *he* was.

And even though his eyes were burning with fatigue after long hours of intense concentration in theatre, he'd never be too exhausted to appreciate a goodlooker. If it came *that* state of affairs — then he'd really see the need to take that break the powers-that-be kept urging on him!

No, he felt quite revived by the sight of her: an attractively uncomplicated girl, hair straight and swinging and that wonderful, carefree stride taking her confidently on her way.

Tom didn't feel like going straight

back to the Manor. It was a twenty-minute drive. After sorting out a burst aneurism spurting its fountain of blood into the faces of the surgical team, he was drained of adrenalin and his back ached like crazy. Crises, though, were part of a working day; brain surgeons worked habitually on the brink of disaster. He'd sleep at the flat tonight.

As the Porsche slid out of the main gates Tom found himself confronted by a video-replay of that unknown girl darting between cars as he'd first caught sight of her.

Hallucination. His own brain now protesting and demanding a break.

He shook his head irritably to clear his vision, only to find Diana's seductive smile on the far side of the windscreen. Good job he wasn't attempting the longer drive, with these two Lorelei conspiring to tantalise him!

It was hard to imagine two more dissimilar females than that nurse and Diana. Diana — groomed for the TV presenter's job she'd been selected for from a throng of highly-qualified women medics. Groomed till she glittered like the small-screen star she'd become, clever and brittle; and unrecognisable as the fellow medical student he'd been infatuated with at university.

The mermaid had leaned over to get something from the back seat of her little car and the shiny fall of hair had curtained her face from view. That was when Tom had lit up a cigarette, allowing himself an excuse to pause. And yes, her features were as gently attractive at closer quarters; pale oval face untouched by cosmetics, clothing plain and dark and chosen for comfort rather than provocation. Great legs, though — for a mermaid.

Diana, now, had been taught how to dress to enhance. On what the television company paid her she could well afford to! Petite and shapely — and with her new-found confidence making the most of it. That thick hair tinted from mouse to Titian, curled and sprayed and unpleasantly brittle to a man's touch. Face painted with a skill that transformed her strong features to an awesome, unrecognisable beauty.

Doesn't need me any more . . .

Tom's mouth twisted bitterly. His right foot stabbed down to send the Porsche surging across amber traffic lights, left hand reaching for the button permanently tuned to Radio Three. Wagnerian opera filled the car through stereo speakers and he winced at the blast of noise.

. . . Financially — or in any other way!

Small wonder that girl tonight had caught his eye and his imagination. It was just another sign that he and Diana had come to the parting of the ways.

* * *

St Joseph's was much like any other Victorian hospital serving a wide range of urban and rural needs, its red-brick mass extended to the limits of the site until the original symmetry was lost among the clutter of new departments.

To reach Accident and Emergency Christie had to pass the low bulk of the Pathology building where ten to one James would still be hard at work, preparing slides and poring over frozen sections sent down from the theatres for investigation; stooped over a mortuary slab or — and Christie mentally crossed fingers for him — squeezing in time for his own small research project in the labs.

She frowned as she remembered the surgeon in the car park. Some of the more frivolous nurses had built Tom Galvan into the hero-figure of St Joseph's.

Oh, granted a neuro-surgeon must be particularly clever, probing and slicing within living brains. But his admirers said Galvan had the lot. Brilliant surgical technique that must have saved hundreds of lives. *And* — they gloated in yearning tones — great face and body to match up with all the rest!

Not fair. He was even nice, the brute — good-humoured and amiable in theatre, calm under the most severe pressure, and apparently without the least desire to play the rôle of doctor-god.

Nurses discussed his physical attractions and his easy manner — as if, mused Christie, as if some good fairy had waved a magic wand at Tom Galvan's christening and bestowed upon him all the most desirable attributes a man who was a doctor could have.

I wonder what he's *really* like? she mused, thrusting her way through swing doors made of some tough murky plastic and directing that characteristic walk towards the locker room.

But on that quizzical note of speculation Tom Galvan disappeared into the realms of the subconscious. For duty now called. And Christie's stomach gave a nervous, preparatory leap.

★　★　★

12

Casualty: the sharp end of the service. Here too, crises were a feature of each working day — if she'd had the option, the last place Christie would have chosen to be a staff nurse on nights.

Newly qualified, and particularly anxious to stay on because of Dr Mallory and because after three deeply satisfying years of training 'Joe's' felt very special to her, RGN Wisdom had gratefully — after a very deep breath — accepted the temporary post of junior staff nurse on Casualty night duty. The long and weary nine till eight shift.

'I'm told y'r heart's in medical nursing,' observed Mrs Harris, the Chief Nursing Officer, in her brisk Scots burr, 'but if you'll bide your time till a staff job comes up at Joseph's, then we'll be glad to interview you for the post.

'I'm not promising ye'll get it, o'course,' she added, peering sagely over her tortoiseshell frames, mighty gratified as the rough-skinned hands clasped in an involuntary anxiety that belied Wisdom's composed expression. St Joseph's would not in all truth — and well Mrs Harris knew it — wish to see this dedicated and selfless RGN follow some of her colleagues to the glamour of London. Utterly reliable. A nurse of integrity.

Perhaps a little over-dedicated, if such a thing were possible. A mite too solemn; hard to imagine this one ever fooling around or giggling on duty . . . Odd background, if Gaynor Harris remembered correctly, some sort of family crisis. Might be an idea to check back in the records one wee moment.

'I can't offer jobs to all you girls when you pass y'r Finals — wish I could! We could use every one of you. But you appreciate that we have to operate on minimum staffing levels. So! Tell me, Wisdom, why d'ye prefer medical nursing to all the other specialities you've experienced during your training?'

Christie swallowed, searching for the

words that would not give the Nursing Officer the wrong impression. For without wishing to offend Mrs Harris, it was Christie's genuine belief that the most satisfying nursing was to be found on the medical wards, where the patients were often very sick and requiring vigilant care. It was hard work, and demanding, of course. Routine, yes, and undramatic. But for Christie that was a vital factor. She'd known enough of drama to last a lifetime.

In the hot seat there in the CNO's office her recollection went into vivid rewind. The sense of blessed relief when her second-year stint in the Accident and Emergency Unit (to give Cas its official title) was over. Nights would be twice as painful.

But Christie's determination to stay on at Joe's was fierce. Oh, by golly! she thought, I'll work night and day on Cas if it'll please the powers that be. I'm well aware my references would land me a post in a famous London teaching hospital — but wild horses couldn't drag me back there.

'Ever since my first year — ' she began earnestly, aware of the tension in her voice easing as she talked on and the growing approval in Mrs Harris's eyes. And she must have come up with something convincing, for next moment she was being directed into the secretary's office and found herself signing a temporary contract, and being ushered out briskly with instructions to go down to the sewing room and get measured for six new uniforms and the pale-blue belt and frilled caps of a staff nurse.

And thus Christie had found herself back among the crises and catastrophes that made up a working night on the Accident and Emergency Unit of St Joseph's.

It wasn't so much fear of the physical danger that bothered Christie Wisdom, though violent attacks upon casualty staff were becoming such a nationwide problem that the Royal College of

Nursing was giving serious consideration to the idea of bodyguards, and Christie was no braver than average. It was that sense of imminent crisis which hung permanently over Cas, an adrenalin-charged atmosphere that many of the staff thrived upon, but which got under Christie's skin and gave her the jitters.

Yes, she knew she could cope as competently as any: outwardly calm and matter-of-fact, helping process patients through the system which admitted them into a hospital bed or despatched them home to lick their wounds. All the same, her fervent prayer was to be taken off Cas at the earliest opportunity.

She'd been working there since early March — almost a month now to get settled into the routine of nights and to feel part and parcel of the friendly team of doctors and nurses.

As usual, on this particular April night, she hung up her cloak and headed along the corridor for the briefing of on-coming night staff over a cup of coffee in Sister's small cubbyhole, tightening her pale-blue petersham belt and dabbing a proud finger at the row of modest frilling round her staff nurse's cap.

'Girding yourself for the fray, Christie?' commented the Casualty Registrar, scrutinising her spectacularly trim waistline.

'Hello, Simon! Are we busy tonight?'

'Not so far, but I never was one for rash predictions. Just off to grab a bite while I have the chance. If you need me send me a postcard.'

With an amused shake of her head Christie glanced back at the disappearing white coat tails. Simon Brownley had once shared a flat with James, but that had been well before she arrived at Joe's. Simon was married now, with twin baby daughters.

After the report, Sister Brenda got on with some paperwork while her staff nurse patrolled the department to make sure they were organised and ready for any emergency.

'Hi there, gorgeous,' teased Mike Filing, the Senior House Officer, creeping up on Staff Nurse Wisdom as she tested the oxygen taps in a treatment room. 'I saw you batting your lovely eyelashes at Simon Brownley!'

'Friend of Dr Mallory's.' Christie hoped she sounded tersely discouraging. She rechecked equipment prepared earlier by the day staff, knowing that nothing was more infuriating than to start an aseptic technique and find no Savlon on the trolley. She removed an empty bottle from an overhead cupboard and added it to the dispensary basket just inside the door.

'You're a fusspot,' scoffed Mike.

'I take my job seriously,' she observed evenly.

'You can say that again, Matron!' grinned Mike gleefully. Ever since the first night she'd reported for duty on A & E — and had the lack of foresight to confide in the apparently friendly and sympathetic SHO she'd been working alongside — he'd been fascinated by the decidedly appealing Staff Nurse Wisdom with her cool manner and unflirtatious ways.

Angel in Disguise, Mike had secretly christened her. If he hadn't heard it from her own lips he'd never have believed it: for Cas terrified the daylights out of this cool and competent new staff nurse!

'So-o-o?' he carried on dramatically, leaning on the door jamb with arms folded, grinning all over that boyish freckled face which had inspired so many unwise confidences in the past. 'Why should Brownley be rewarded with smiles, when all *I* get is frozen glares? See, you're doing it now! Fighting against that surge of overwhelming desire you feel for me . . . Know what you are, Christie Wisdom? You're an Angel in Disguise.'

The girl's look of alarm was quite startling in its unexpectedness. Mike stopped in his tracks . . . then recovered impetus, raving on about Christie being a woman of hidden depths; on the surface so grave and cool, underneath it all, a volcano about to jettison that boring twit Mallory and explode with passion for one Dr Filing.

As swiftly the troubled pallor was replaced by Christie's usual calm. She even managed a half-hearted smile, for Mike's nightly declarations of ardour were rather flattering. And it was only in the slow periods that he succeeded in making a nuisance of himself with these amorous charades. Anyway, it was her own fault. That first night on Cas when her defences were down, she'd made a stupid admission of frailty she was not to be allowed to forget.

Mike followed her into the sluice and Christie found herself trapped in a corner by the sink clutching an armful of grey papier mâché vomit bowls. Pointedly she sighed and checked her fob watch, waiting with patient dignity for Mike to get bored and abandon the Warren Beatty performance for another night and tolerating with downcast eyes his minute perusal of her face.

In self-derision Mike heard himself spouting a load of nonsense into the delicate whorl of her ear. But it was the effect she had on him! He knew he was behaving like an idiot and simply annoying her. His breath beat upon the porcelain-clear skin as he bent towards her — a tall girl, almost as tall as he.

'If you . . . if you did your eyes up a bit — you know, some of that black stuff — and some pink on your cheeks. Oh boy, you'd look really something!'

Ridiculous. The girl looked great just as she was, in spite of the severity of her hairdo — a tautly efficient style which swept every hair back off her face into a neat figure of eight at the nape of her fragile neck.

Tall, slender, neat-featured — why, she could make herself look as good as a *Vogue* model if she only had the know-how, reckoned Mike appraisingly. Not that she'd get much encouragement from James Mallory. Decent fellow, of course, but one of those non-communicating pathologists who hide away in laboratories because they can't cope with real live people . . . How the *hell* did these two get involved in the first place?

'Oh, there you are, Mike!' came a plaintive voice from the doorway, 'I've been looking for you everywhere.'

It was the buxom young medical student from Leeds, mask dangling beneath her chin; trying valiantly to get in extra clinical experience at St Joseph's during the Easter vacation — under the guidance of the elusive Dr Filing.

With an audible groan Mike dashed a hand through his untidy mop of reddish curls. 'Sorry, Janet. I forgot I'd promised to check those stitches you put in.'

The girl seemed blithely unaware of having interrupted Dr Filing's bizarre mating ritual. 'I *told* you I'd been invited to a party in one of the Nurses' Homes,' she complained. 'Now it's too late for me to go home and change.'

Thoughtfully the three of them

regarded scarlet leg warmers atop blue suede ankle boots, incongruous beneath a white medical coat.

'Go barefoot,' suggested Christie helpfully. 'Those nurses' rooms are far too hot.'

'There won't be any lights on anyway,' added Mike, 'no one will see what you're wearing. Might pop across myself at the midnight hour — '

Christie made good her escape.

★ ★ ★

Emergency!

The red phone had a direct line linking St Joseph's with the ambulance station. Its urgent message shrilled through the department.

Christie — nearest member of the team — had her hand on the receiver within seconds. She'd long dreaded its warning of battered and broken bodies being conveyed by speeding ambulance direct to the Unit for help.

She would never forget the horror of

that summer's day when she had wrung her hands over her father's body, ignorant of the techniques that would have pulled him through the crisis.

Here she stood, four years later, equipped and ready to cope. She had the necessary skills, could help save lives, and hand and voice were steady and confident. It wasn't so bad after all, being back on Casualty.

Dad would be proud of you, Christie Wisdom! she congratulated herself in a fleeting moment of fierce pride, pushing the crackling receiver against her ear. You really *are* a true professional — not an 'angel in disguise', dressed up as a nurse but pretending all the while.

'St Joseph's. Accident and Emergency.'

★   ★   ★

The staff nurse's ear received the terse message with alert detachment: three minutes warning of a bad RTA being brought in from the bypass motorway.

Simon Brownley, the Resident Surgical Officer, was back from supper but busy in theatre patching up a teenage motor-cyclist with a number of nasty, though not disabling, injuries.

'Sue, get Mike Filing!' Christie called urgently to a third-year nurse who had heard the emergency phone and was holding aside the curtains of the cubicle in which she'd been dressing a cut-and-stitched thumb. 'RTA, one man — multiple injuries. Arriving in two minutes!'

As the ambulance raced up to the emergency doors Christie was ready and waiting, glancing back anxiously over her shoulder for reinforcements. The ambulance crew would have done all they could as trained paramedics, but right now that patient needed a doctor! Where the hell had Mike got to? Surely everyone must have been alerted by the shrill bell of the emergency phone?

'No one else involved, Ned?' she questioned breathlessly as the driver of the ambulance ran round to open up the rear doors for her to board.

Ned Piggott shook his head, his face unusually grim. 'Poor devil must've fallen asleep at the wheel, hit one of the motorway bridges. They work too damn 'ard, our doctors. Brace yourself, Staff! You're in for a shock. We've got Mr Galvan in here!'

The world spun.

Then a sort of frozen professionalism urged Christie to her patient's side. Only the thick black curls were just about recognisable beneath a film of pale dust that must have showered Tom Galvan when he smashed into the concrete obstruction. He didn't seem to be wearing his thick overcoat. His face was a mess of bloody lacerations. The features could have belonged to anyone.

'You're *sure* it's Mr Galvan?' There was a shudder in Christie's voice as she forced her mind's eye to drop the shutters over the image of the tall handsome neurosurgeon, strong and healthy and at the height of his physical and intellectual powers, sombrely shrugged into his heavy black overcoat.

Tim O'Reilly winced at the memory of that tangle of red twisted metal. Mr Galvan had operated on his father-in-law once — removed a clot from his brain and made a new man of him. His voice was choked with emotion. 'Soon as I saw the wrecked Porsche, I knew. Mary and all the saints! I thought to meself, not *him*, not Tom Galvan.'

At this, though to all appearances unconscious, the injured man groaned. Christie remembered that the sense of hearing remained acute even in those close to death. She put her finger to her lips.

The crew had seen to the basics, checking the airway and keeping Tom Galvan, who was suffering from severe shock, warm beneath a space blanket. Carefully Christie exposed the upper body, noting the evidence of traumatic injury: left arm oddly distorted and clutched across the chest in such a way that it was impossible to gauge the damage to heart or lungs.

That was definitely a grunt of protest.

'Won't let us near that arm, Staff.'

As if he comprehended what was being said Tom Galvan sighed and muttered, and it seemed to Christie that an almost subliminal determination on the injured doctor's part held his shattered arm immobile. Chill droplets of perspiration beaded his forehead mingling with the cuts and dirt. Reaching beneath the blanket, she noted the cold clammy feel of hands and feet, the racing, thready pulse reflecting a heart struggling to circulate its diminishing supplies of blood.

An icy desperate calm took hold of her as her worst fears were realised. Somewhere deep within there must be haemorrhage, the silent unseen oozing of blood into the cavities of the body.

'BP a hundred over sixty,' volunteered O'Reilly. 'Pulse a hundred and fifty and rising.'

Christie nodded, her face stiff with tension. In the absence of a doctor it was up to her to assess Mr Galvan's most urgent needs . . . A low reading, to be sure, but as yet not disastrous. Blood pressure is resilient, she reminded herself, the last thing to go. But when it can hold out no longer the drop will be sudden and Tom Galvan will be only minutes from death.

As she replaced the blanket her fingers grazed the damaged arm and the man's lips moved in silent protest. Gently she touched the swollen hand in comforting reassurance. 'No one is going to move your arm.' She spoke very distinctly, bending close to his ear.

Another sigh escaped the bruised lips and he drifted deeper into unconsciousness.

The ambulance crew were not in the least offended by this angry and curt young staff nurse issuing orders right left and centre. They quite agreed: where the hell *were* all the bloody doctors? Yes, they would transfer their gravely injured patient with due care and speed to the Emergency Room, while Christie Wisdom personally dragged the duty surgeon screaming and kicking out of theatre!

Hard-bitten after years of experience, O'Reilly and Piggott looked grimly at each other.

They sympathised with the nurse's desperation. It *was* unthinkable. But when the chips were down even a neuro-surgeon was only human.

And they both knew the score.

This one wasn't going to make it. No one could save Tom Galvan now.

2

The senior consultant in General Surgery pulled a handkerchief from the breast pocket of his velvet smoking jacket and mopped his brow in irritation. Wretched woman, interrupting his evening with her neurotic bowels! But Night Sister had been right to call him; it might have turned out to be an early obstruction, and Mrs Hawkesley-Gurridge (he deserved a medal for getting that mouthful right) was paying the earth to be sure of Sir Frank Davy's personal attention.

And St Joseph's benefited, Frank saw to that. Since his wife had died and his children flown to nests of their own, there was no longer any real need to augment his hospital salary by taking on private patients. His own wants were simple enough. This jacket, for instance, would see him out.

Lulu had bought all his clothes. Her taste was impeccable — and a good job! for it was Frank's proud boast that he possessed none. A rough diamond, he liked to call himself, a boyo from the Welsh valleys who had made good.

'Sir Frank' this and 'Sir Frank' that — Mrs H-G made very free with the damn title. He'd never looked for honours, never. But the kids had been thrilled, bless 'em all three. Not to speak of his seven grandchildren.

If only Lulu *cariad* had lived to enjoy all the fuss! Antoinette, her real name was, and she'd been the daughter of the first consultant he had worked for. To a lad from a Welsh coalmining village it sounded like foreign: so he'd called her Lulu as a joke, and the name had stuck.

He'd been lonely since she died.

For a man of his age Sir Frank was in fair shape. Ignoring the lift, he came down the flights of stairs leading to the main foyer of the Nazareth private wing, nimble-footed in his black patent evening shoes. It was surgery that kept him so spry at sixty-three. Not one of them had dared hint at the looming spectre of Frank Davy's retirement . . . yet! Let 'em dare. 'Goodnight, Boddington.'

The night porter had heard him coming and held the double glass doors wide in readiness. 'Goodnight to you, Sir Frank.'

A shallow bank of steps flanked the entrance and lent a certain grandeur to the private wing. Sir Frank paused there while he pulled string-backed driving gloves over small deft hands, filling his lungs with a deep draught of mild April air. The last niggle of irritation wafted away on a gentle breeze now teasingly revealing the bald spot in his thick grey hair. Definitely a touch of spring tonight. Pity he'd had to refuse the chance of a coffee with that charming Night Sister upstairs . . . one gloved hand smoothed the hair back into place.

Ah, vanity! thought Sir Frank rue-fully. Spring is in the air and the pineal gland hard at work getting lads and lasses in the mood for love. A night when anything could happen, except to old codgers like me. Now shall I skip that boring charade Sister Lewis released me from, and take her up on the coffee, or shall I get off home to bed and hope she'll call me out again later? A vision of curly white hair and merry hazel eyes in a youthful unlined face filled his mind's eye with temptation.

'So sorry to interrupt your evening,' she had said pleasantly, but with a twinkle that suggested she quite enjoyed rescuing consultants from tedious dinner parties. He'd heard a rumour that she wasn't married — widowed or divorced or something. Lewis — could be Welsh even. Good-looking enough, at any rate. He suddenly remembered the pudding he was missing out on — raspberry Pavlova, and dammit, his hostess must have made it because she knew it was his favourite.

The Bentley was parked close by.

Elderly but well-preserved, mused Sir Frank fondly, and that goes for the two of us. Never given me a moment's trouble, have you, old lass?

He checked the clock on the polished walnut dash-board. Might as well head back for his share of pudding. The engine purred as if it ran on cream.

Within the hospital grounds Sir Frank drove slowly, taking the narrow roadways and blind corners with meticulous care and a watchful eye for dark-cloaked figures scurrying between wards and dining room. Past the mortuary and the path. labs and the hospital's small chapel . . .

'What the devil?'

Out of the shadows the slim form of a nurse raced into his path, arms wildly waving, grasping the handle even as he slowed to a halt, wrenching his driver's door open and urgently clutching at his velvet sleeve.

'Sir Frank — it *is* you — I saw the Bentley . . . oh, you must please come! Mr Galvan's been hurt — we may be too late. But if anyone can save him it's you!'

The words tumbled from Christie's lips in an urgent gabble, but with immediate effect. For, abandoning his vehicle right where it was, the great man followed hot on her heels as the desperate staff nurse raced back into the bright lights of Casualty.

Much later, biting her lip at her own temerity, Christie could hardly believe what she'd done. All but *dragged* Sir Frank Davy out of his Bentley — leaving it to jam up the hospital's thoroughfare! — getting him to Tom Galvan's side about thirty seconds before the SHO himself arrived on the scene to get the pasting of his career.

Heedless of his immaculate cuffs, the head of General Surgery had at the speed of light assessed Tom's injuries; calling down, as he worked, the wrath of the Almighty upon every doctor within scolding distance.

And at this point Mike rolled up: he'd been genuinely detained with another emergency, but this didn't save him from the great man's blistering Welsh tongue. 'Blithering idiots, the lot of you!' he was storming in a general description that included every member of the Casualty team including Christie herself — and quite deservingly, she was agreeing silently as she cut away Tom Galvan's clothing and prepared him for surgery.

'I find Tom Galvan in a state of shock and completely unattended! Now get him into theatre *immediately*, d'you hear?'

'Yes, sir.' The SHO's freckled face was grimly adult, no trace of boyishness now. Sue, the third-year, rushed up with a giving set for Dr Filing to administer the fluids Sir Frank had demanded. Christie ripped open the sterile pack while Sue hurried off to bring a drip stand.

'Haven't you got that drip up *yet*?'

'Just — er — seeing to it, sir,' muttered Mike, struggling to find a vein in Tom Galvan's right arm.

'Sir Frank!' interrupted Christie, her voice harsh with urgency. For even as the riot act was being read over him, Tom Galvan's face was altering to an ominous pallor.

'Hell!' muttered the surgeon beneath his breath as his experienced clinical eye warned that Galvan had perhaps two minutes to live. He wrenched off his jacket and rolled his sleeves up tight over surprisingly strong-looking forearms. No time for niceties like theatre pyjamas. And it wouldn't be the first time he'd operated in his shirt sleeves.

'He needs blood. Five units immediately and probably another ten pints to come. Staff Nurse — I want two more giving sets and two drip stands, and on the double. We'll give him the blood twice as fast.'

The Welsh voice was calm. He might have been ordering the day's milk supply. Christie moved like greased lightning.

'And *you*, boyo,' continued Sir Frank, breathing down Dr Filing's neck, 'if he's not on the table and ready for me in seconds, I shall have y'r guts for garters.'

Now it was Mike's turn to blench.

The duty registrar came bursting into the emergency theatre, his white coat spattered with dark red spots, face shocked and anxious.

'Ah, Brownley,' observed Sir Frank with ominous sing-song calm. 'Good of you to pop in and see us.'

'Appalling!' Mr Brownley was shaking his head over the unconscious neuro-surgeon. 'When I heard the news I could scarcely believe it. One hell of a decent bloke.' He came round to the far side of the table and peered at the more obvious injuries, whistled through his teeth. 'Lord! I don't like the look of that. What are you going to tackle first, Sir Frank?'

Christie, who had scrubbed and gowned with more haste than judgement, stood shivering over the instruments trolley. She fixed her eyes on Mr Galvan's face as if committing every inch of torn and bruised flesh and bone to memory. In fact she was trying to relate this battered mess with the unsettlingly handsome face she remembered in the car park. With half of her concentration she picked up fragments of what the two surgeons were discussing . . . shattered arm . . . miracle . . . smallest movement could have sent a sliver of bone ripping through the main artery to the left hand . . .

Simon Brownley's lean face looked grave. 'D'you think he can make it?' he questioned, stepping nimbly out of the elder surgeon's way, his voice glum with doubt.

'Not if we stand around gossiping. Now make yourself useful, Mr Brownley — get a haematology technician to come in and crossmatch that blood immediately.'

'I'll see to it.'

'Good man.' The adrenal glands were already responding to the excitement of challenge, pouring their secretions into the surgeon's blood-stream as he extended a gloved hand for the first instrument. The surge of adrenalin drove the last thought of raspberry Pavlova from Sir Frank's keenly concentrating brain.

'We shall pull our patient through!' he pronounced to his team with a grand and confident optimism.

And behind her mask Staff Nurse Wisdom held her breath. She was banking on it.

* * *

Going off duty next morning Christie was surprised to hear herself hailed in the main entrance hall — by none other than the great man himself. Sir Frank had been making a visit to Intensive Care before starting the day's theatre list.

He was smiling. No need to ask why. 'And if it hadn't been for you, young lady, I shouldn't be looking so pleased with myself. I've been up to ICU and you'll be relieved to know our patient is still holding his own. Sent a rocket round your department, mind you, but it turns out no one was to blame. Brownley was dealing with an obstetric emergency, and that whipper-snapper SHO — forget exactly what his excuse was, but it held water. More hands on deck, that's what they could do with in A & E! What did you say your name was again? Christie Wisdom?'

Wisdom — now that rings a bell, mused Sir Frank, noting the dark circles under Christie's big brown eyes and the drained pallor of her skin. But of course it couldn't be . . . Archie Wisdom's daughter would never have trained in a provincial hospital; she'd be at Guy's or Tommy's, sticking with the London scene.

'Away to your bed, Nurse Wisdom. That was quite a night! A race against time! I don't mind admitting it now, see. But if we'd lost Tom I should never have forgiven myself. Never mind, lots of TLC and he'll be good as new.'

Christie heaved a mighty sigh of relief to hear it. Her sudden smile was so enchanting that Sir Frank mentally revised his first impression of her as a rather prim-looking young woman.

'I'm just starting my nights off,' she explained, 'so I'm in no particular hurry to get home to bed.' Not really wanting to leave the hospital at all, she thought wistfully; I'm like an actor hyped up after a demanding performance, staving off the oblivion of sleep. Yet my bones truly do ache with weariness.

He patted her bare arm. And the eyes of those who passed along the corridor gleamed with curiosity, for elderly consultants did not, as a rule, chat up junior staff nurses in public places . . . Then they remembered the latest gossip on the hospital grapevine and put two and two together: of course! Christie Wisdom — the one who'd hurled herself in front of Sir Frank Davy's Bentley and helped save Tom Galvan's life in the drama of the decade.

Just as she was on the point of leaving, Christie changed her mind and headed for the lift. Her four nights off meant there wouldn't be an opportunity to keep tabs on Mr Galvan's progress. She'd dearly like to slip up to Intensive Care and see with her own eyes that all was well — as well as could be expected considering the gravity of the worst of his injuries, the torn liver and the shattered arm.

But they were very busy in the Unit, and Christie realised this was not the most convenient moment to interrupt the day staff and ask for a progress report. Peering through the glass screens, she could see that seven of the ten beds were occupied, each surrounded by its quota of the sort of machinery that figured in a layman's nightmare visions. Seven people who were very ill indeed. But which one was her man?

The level of heat was getting to her, and she winced at the trickle of sweat stealing down between her shoulder-blades and the constriction in her throat as if she too breathed only with difficulty.

Nothing for it but to go on home. Her shoulders drooped in weary disappointment at not even having managed a glimpse of Tom Galvan.

Come off it, Wisdom, she scolded herself. You can't afford to get wound up about patients; a nurse would soon crack up if she didn't exercise some self-control.

Just then, one of the masked and gowned nurses moved aside, and there Tom lay, attached to all manner of equipment. Christie's tired eyes noted IV infusions, a urinary catheter, electro-encephalogram monitoring brain activity; and Tom himself — at such a time she couldn't think of him as Mr Galvan, the invulnerable professional — covered only by a sheet from under which clear plastic tubes snaked down into Redi-vac containers already filling with the seepage of blood-stained fluids draining from the liver repair.

Thank God he was breathing for himself and seemed to be in a drugged post-operative sleep, his face partially obscured by the naso-gastric tube taped across his left cheek.

'Looking for someone?' demanded a sarcastic voice.

Christie started involuntarily, glancing round for the briefest instant in apparent guilt. With a will of their own her eyes travelled back to Tom Galvan's still form.

The frowning anaesthetist clicked her tongue impatiently. Goodness, she hoped they weren't going to have lovesick nurses trooping in and out all day to gawp at the hospital's heartthrob. But her expression cleared when this drained, ashen-faced staff nurse explained apologetically that she'd been there when they operated on Mr Galvan and she'd popped up for a moment to see how he was.

'Bit of an alarming sight at the moment, of course,' acknowledged the doctor, 'but that's just superficial bruising and oedema, as you know, and in a few days his face will be beautiful as ever.' The girl couldn't even raise a ghost of a smile. 'Got two lovely black eyes . . . must have had quite a whack on the head, but we're monitoring that and it's pretty certain everything's OK up top. Come up any time,' she suggested generously. 'Of course he's not out of the woods yet, and I shouldn't like to be there when he realises that arm's been well and truly plastered.'

'Thank goodness it was his left,' sighed Christie in weary relief.

'Didn't you know?' The anaesthetist raised expressive eyebrows. 'Tom Galvan's a southpaw. God knows what this is going to do to his career.'

★ ★ ★

Dr Mallory would be coming over for supper and an evening of TV. The customary arrangement when Christie started her nights off: unoriginal, perhaps, but both were tired and perfectly content to make it a quiet night beside her glowing log fire.

On her way home, Christie stopped at the shopping centre to stock up with eggs and cheese and plenty of fresh fruit and vegetables. She normally found enough second wind to keep going till late morning and a three-hour nap. James was not particularly keen on meat, and as a matter of convenience Christie shared his preferences.

Well, it does us both good to eat sensibly, she agreed, pushing a laden trolley round Sainsburys. Regretfully she shook her head over a pack of juicy hunks of fillet steak which in a moment of weakness and fatigue caught her eye. She popped into Ye Olde Bakehouse for a malted whole-grain bloomer, then, weariness catching up with her, yawned in the post office queue for the weekly aerogramme she sent off to Zurich.

When at last she reached home her heart gave a jump at finding a chunky-looking letter face-down on the doormat. She dropped her parcels and with fumbling fingers tore it open on the instant. Photographs, wonderful photographs. Pictures that turned her heart over . . . and a letter that began: 'Christie darling, more for your albums. I never want you to feel Ben is growing up a stranger to you. As you see, your Easter egg caused enormous pleasure and even more mess! Yes, he's so much like his father and that is understandably painful for you. But, Christie, I see so much of *you* in Ben too . . . '

★　★　★

James had a heavy cold, expressing — between noisy sessions with a voluminous handkerchief — grave concern over Tom Galvan's catastrophe.

Though Christie made light of her own part in the drama, news had raced through St Joseph's with the speed of a forest fire.

'And Sir Frank whipped off his

smoking jacket and plunged straight in!' recalled Christie admiringly. 'He was just incredible. He saved a life when everything seemed hopeless. Oh, James! I can't begin to tell you the *relief* I felt when Tom Galvan was taken up to Intensive Care. I could have cried! My eyes were full of tears.'

Though the pathologist considered such emotion extravagant in a trained nurse, he'd grown too fond of Christie to wish to hurt her feelings by saying so. There was a pause while James cleared his throat and searched around for a suitable comment.

'I expect you were exhausted,' he murmured, delving through his pockets for a clean handkerchief. 'I don't like the sound of that shattered humerus. Neurosurgery's a tricky field: Galvan may never operate again.'

Christie bit her lip, frowning as she remembered the gaffe she'd made over that business of the left arm. Well, she'd assumed Mr Galvan was right-handed. How her newly buoyant spirits had plummeted when the doctor on Intensive Care dropped the bombshell.

'And a ruptured liver — hmmm.' James's intake of breath hissed through his teeth. 'Galvan's going to be hors de combat for some while. God help his department. They'll have to send the really tricky stuff to Murray over at Southampton. I suppose if all goes well they'll transfer him to the Nazareth Wing, and then he'll be convalescent for a couple of months.'

'Let's have supper,' sighed Christie, 'and talk of something more cheerful.'

She vanished into her little kitchen — all white walls and white surfaces and as clinically functional as any hospital theatre — and within three minutes food was on the dining room table. This room was as unfussy as the rest of the house — no clutter, no ornaments, no pictures, no family photographs. Just white pottery bowls of shiny-leaved green house plants to relieve the severity of black-stained wood. It was interesting, thought James, taking his seat at the head of the table, that Christie's home was so indicative of her state of mind. Severe, almost; nothing without purpose. A total rejection of what her privileged upbringing must have been like.

'This soup's good! Did you make it?'

'Mmm — Delia Smith's leek and potato. Want some more?' As she spooned a second generous helping from the saucepan, the lenses of James's steel-framed specs steamed up. With solemn care Christie wiped them on her linen napkin and stuck them back on his beaky nose. Behind the fresh-polished lenses his short-sighted grey eyes, red-rimmed with rheum, smiled his thanks.

His cold seemed a little better after the hearty bowls of soup. 'For a gal who could just about scramble an egg last year,' commented Christie with satisfaction, 'that was not half bad.' She disappeared through the stripped-pine door, to return bearing dishes of sliced tomatoes (sprinkled with fresh basil from the collection of herbs over-wintering in terracotta pots on the kitchen sill) and a golden-topped macaroni cheese spiked with crispy bacon and slivers of fried onion, the final touch a green salad glossy with walnut-oil dressing.

Pudding was a bowl of sweet clementines, which Christie peeled for James as they sprawled comfortably by the fireside in her sitting room, James in a downy-cushioned chair with peach linen covers, Christie curled at his feet on the coral Afghan rug, resting her head against his knobbly cavalry-twill knees. Not too close to James because, as he sensibly pointed out, she didn't want to risk catching his cold.

It was good to have him there, relaxed and more at ease in her little home with each visit he made. Christie would have loved to suggest he moved in with her — but when she'd once ventured a hint he'd looked so worried that she'd never mentioned the subject again. It was enough for him to have come to terms with the idea of her being able to afford to live independently. He was so sensible, so reliably down to earth: the kind of man who roused Christie's instinct to cuddle and care for with his penchant for shabby corduroy jackets and check Viyella shirts, his soft mousy hair clipped close about his ears and neatly parted.

'Might be an idea . . . ' began James, measuring his words with the same meticulous care he was devoting to removing every shred of white pith from a segment of clementine. 'Might be an idea if I kept a pair of slippers here.' His hands were quite beautiful, the fingers long and tapering.

Christie stared at those hands as if they could express what was going on in their owner's mind. Was this James's sweet but inarticulate way of coming up — at last — with a proposal of marriage? And why was she suddenly unsure of what her own response should be?

'Mmm,' she agreed in what she

hoped was a suitably encouraging but noncommittal fashion, leaning forward to toss pungent scraps of peel among the crackling applewood logs.

Today James's socks were fawn and green. 'I get a bit of trouble with my circulation,' he confided, wriggling his woollen toes. 'Chilblains — itch like the devil.' He always insisted on leaving his polished brogues in the porch and padding about in diamond-patterned socks. It was sweet of him, but quite unnecessary, for Christie valued people far more highly than cream wool carpets.

'Oh, James,' she chided, 'why didn't you tell me this before? Oh, and look at your elbows, they're almost worn through! I'm going to fetch my sewing basket immediately.'

In spite of his protests the fawn pullover came off and was returned five minutes later with a deftly woven darn. 'There!' teased Christie, knowing how fussy James was about neatness, 'you'd need a microscope to spot that.' Emboldened, she loosened his university-crested tie to half-mast, happily content to be playing mother in her quiet little home.

James would have kissed her but for his germs. Instead he patted her hand, noticing how chapped and sore it was. 'You're a funny girl,' he said affectionately. 'With all the money your father left you, you don't need to work. Yet not only do you earn your own living but you choose the most arduous profession possible.'

Christie said nothing. James too fell silent. He had his own theories, but putting them into words was something he'd never been good at. Four years had passed since her father's sudden and traumatic death. Casualty, in James's opinion, was the worst place for Christie: a continual reminder. Working there must feel like probing into a slow-healing wound.

'Any A and E unit is a stressful environment for nursing staff. Last night must have been difficult for you — one of our own doctors, and so gravely injured.'

Christie was blinking back the tears and couldn't trust herself to speak. Such demonstrations of understanding showed James for the genuine person he really was, gentle and considerate and kind. It wasn't true, that cheap jibe of Dr Filing's about pathologists being cold and uncommunicative, and preferring snips of tissue on slides to real live human beings.

Last night! . . . it was dawning on her now, with a dizzy sense of relief, that last night she had passed some manner of self-imposed test; had successfully cleared the hurdle that had made emergency nursing a source of anxious fears.

'I wonder — ' began James hesitantly, his expression troubled as he regarded Christie's bowed head. Sometimes she seemed so alone in the world, so vulnerable.

She looked about fifteen tonight, with her long brown hair in a ponytail, jeans that ended above fragile ankles and narrow-boned feet in black pumps.

He rested a concerned hand upon her shoulder, feeling tension in the delicate bones beneath the white cotton shirt.

'I wonder, would it help if I spoke to the Chief Nursing Officer and explained the position?'

The heavy ponytail whipped left, then right in vigorous protest. 'Dear James, you mustn't worry about me, really and truly. You see — ' she added slowly, 'what happened last night was very important in . . . in a way I'm not sure I can put my finger on yet. The only way to describe it is to say that I feel as if I've passed some sort of test. And now the L-plates are off!'

'Yes, that's it.' Her voice held the low thrill of relief. No more pretending to be a fully fledged angel. The L-plates were off. Christie Alice Wisdom could cope with just about anything: a *proper* Casualty staff nurse from this day on.

She scrambled to her knees and squeezed James's two hands, her eye falling on his gold wristwatch. 'Your Western film's on in five minutes.' Her warm smile dazzled his eyes. 'Pour yourself a cognac, darling, while I see to the coffee.'

★ ★ ★

Back on duty the following week, Christie enquired if Sister Brenda had news of Mr Galvan's progress. James was away attending a two-day course in Southampton, so she'd heard no hospital bulletins but was anticipating that all would be well.

It had been clear to Christie when preparing Tom Galvan's unconscious body for emergency surgery that he must in the normal run of things be particularly fit and healthy. He possessed the sort of strongly muscled olive-skinned physique that even an athlete would be proud to own. If he pulled through . . . for a moment Christie held her breath in silent prayer. If he pulled through, then his recovery ought to be remarkably swift: strong body coupled with a strong will to throw off physical incapacity. Draping his nakedness with sterile towels, she had hesitated, biting her lip beneath the mask that concealed all but her wide brown eyes, pupils darkly dilated. Not if, but when. *When* Tom Galvan came safely through surgery his positive attitude to recovery would make him the perfect patient.

The Day Sister's initial hesitation was therefore a bit odd. And Christie thought her expression was peculiar, too — as if Sister wanted to warn her about something, but knew she couldn't.

'Mr Galvan? Well, dear, I understand everything's — er — satisfactory. And of course he's such a big strong chap, isn't he, and that's always a plus. And Sir Frank's giving him the VIP treatment, as you'd expect. It's only natural that . . . '

'Ah, Brenda! You're still here.'

Simon Brownley breezed into the office, filling its cramped space with the vigorous odour of Hibiscrub, and whatever it was Sister had been about to divulge got lost in an urgent discussion that did not concern Christie.

She, having more than enough to get on with, beat a hasty retreat. And it was only in the canteen at one a.m. that the latest rumour on the grapevine reached her disbelieving ears.

'Brain damage!'

'That's what I said — *brain* damage!' insisted Sharon Collis, a good-looking blonde staff nurse from Obs. and Gynae. who had once been taken to a doctors' party by Tom Galvan — a brief fling that never got off the ground for reasons the self-centred Sharon never had managed to fathom.

'Sort of ironical, isn't it — for a *neuro*-surgeon. Surely you've heard? Oh no, of course, you've been off. Didn't your James tell you?' she added curiously.

Christie's manner sometimes disconcerted colleagues. Behind her back, some gossiped that she was stand-offish and aloof, that it was only normal to be interested in what everyone else was up to.

Collis would have loved to get hold of some delicious titbit concerning Wisdom to spread around St Joseph's. Second best was this intriguing chance to ruffle Wisdom's smooth feathers, observe with spiteful satisfaction that high clear brow furrow in alarm, two spots of colour appearing like splodges in a magic painting book on Wisdom's pale cheeks.

She's just like the rest of them — mad about the gorgeous Galvan! crowed Collis to herself, blissfully unaware of the way her malicious thoughts dulled the sparkle of her wide blue eyes: eyes beautiful enough to attract men but not keep them. Not that *I* think Tom Galvan's anything special, but then I've had more chance to find out what he's really like. A snob, that's what. Ordinary nurses aren't good enough for him now he's got the notorious Dr Diamond into bed!

'Oh yes,' she said aloud in drawling tones that attracted the attention of the group of nurses seated at the long refectory table, 'it's true, isn't it, girls? They've decided Tom Galvan must have bashed his head in that car smash, speeding down the motorway for another h-o-t session with Diana Diamond.'

'That's impossible,' retorted Christie sharply, pushing aside her plate of rapidly congealing beef stew, appetite completely gone. 'I took him to X-ray myself. There was no head injury of any significance.'

'Maybe he's developed a clot,' suggested someone.

Heads in white caps swivelled back to Staff Nurse Wisdom, who was biting her lip in evident dismay.

Sharon Collis made a fresh bid for the limelight, announcing self-importantly that she'd overheard two Ward Sisters discussing the surgeon-patient. 'Seems he's been carrying on like a raging bull since they transferred him from Intensive Care to a private room on Nazareth. Sounds like brain damage to me. Can anyone imagine our charming, gallant head of neuro-surgery carrying on like that? The mind boggles!'

'Cerebral injuries can give rise to major alterations in personality,' put in a male nurse self-importantly. 'I've had quite a lot of psychiatric experience, and let me tell you — '

Christie had had enough. Her chair scraped across vinyl tiles as she rose hurriedly to her feet, pulling her cloak across her shoulders. 'Time I went back.'

'I'll walk across with you,' said Helen Anstey, who had to pass Casualty to get to the geriatric block. Outside the two nurses shivered in the biting wind. 'It's gone much colder. This is the bit I don't like — trudging back to the ward on my own in the dead of night.'

'I'll be g-g-glad to be on days again,' confessed Christie, her teeth beginning to chatter in spite of the red-lined woollen cloak. 'I don't think my system adapts well to working nights. I never seem to have any appetite.' She'd eaten very little of her meal and almost nothing since midday but a cup of tea and a sandwich.

Maybe I'm just a little lightheaded — and imagined it, she thought. 'All that rubbish about Galvan's serious head injuries!' she gasped, grabbing on to her hat with one hand as the wind snatched at it.

Helen's next words dispelled that hopeful illusion. 'One of the girls on my corridor is working days up there.' She nodded up at the tall block of the private wing. 'Came off duty *crying* this evening. She'd been told to special Galvan, but he'd been so awful to her she swore she wasn't going back. And apparently the agency nurses are scared stiff of him — and you know what they are, they just don't turn up if they don't fancy the job.'

Christie raised her eyebrows — she'd never nursed private patients and felt rather sorry for those who must.

She couldn't help wondering behind which of those darkened windows lay the dynamic Mr Galvan. And did he sleep sweetly, or toss and fret in his prison of a hospital bed . . .

'I don't know about *brain* damage, though,' mused Helen. 'Sharon Collis is a right little stirrer. But when I said to Carol it was hard to imagine Tom Galvan being so — well — *difficult*, Carol told me it's like nursing Dr Jekyll!' She nudged Christie with a friendly elbow and added, 'No one making that much trouble can be dying, can they!'

They both chuckled, and Christie said she'd always had the impression that Tom Galvan was very popular and well liked. Of course she knew him by sight, and to be sure he was an extremely attractive man. Till the night of his accident she'd never even spoken to him.

'Everyone's heard about you saving his life. That was what was making

Sharon so ratty tonight.'

'R-rubbish! It was Sir Frank Davy who did *that*! Here's my destination — if you're scared I'll walk with you as far as that corner, then I'll watch till I see you go inside your block.'

'That's decent of you, Christie. It's stupid, I know, but the grounds seem so creepy in the lamplight. Do you blame me?'

'No, I don't! These days it seems risky to walk anywhere alone at night. Now off you go.'

Shivering there in the east wind, Christie saw the senior of the team of Night Sisters bustling across from the main building to start her two-a.m. rounds of the sleeping wards. 'Hello, Sister, are you coming to us first?' asked Christie, ready to accompany Sister Roper on the brief visit that would suffice for Casualty.

'Message for you, my dear. Can you pop along to Mrs Harris's office in the morning before you go off duty?'

'Of course, Sister,' said Christie, her

heart leaping with joy and relief at the long-awaited summons. She had shown herself willing, proved she wouldn't refuse any work offered, and now her chance had materialised! A staff job must have come up on one of the medical wards. And Nurse Wisdom, RGN, was considered a worthy candidate: Mrs Harris was about to invite her to apply . . .

For a *permanent* post at St Joseph's!

3

'Hell's teeth, woman!'

The bellow was accompanied by the muffled crash of a tray hitting carpet tiles, the clatter of spilled cutlery and china.

The door of Room 27 burst open and an agitated figure — cap awry, mouth tremulous — tottered breathlessly on the threshold, a spreading dark stain disfiguring her white skirts. From the interior of the private room, a full-throated masculine roar was criticising the quality of breakfasts served to the privileged patients of St Joseph's Nazareth Wing.

'Is it too much to expect a decent cup of coffee while I'm incarcerated in here? And how many more times have I to tell you people: *no* fried muck!'

Something thudded against the far side of the half-open door.

The petrified nurse unfroze and grabbed the handle, putting solid wood between herself and danger. For a moment she leaned against the wall pressing an agitated hand to her damp brow, pausing till fright reduced to manageable proportions.

Then she gave in her notice and left.

*   *   *

'I'm sorry to be asking you to change about like this, Nurse Wisdom. But you'll appreciate that we have a very difficult situation over on Nazareth Wing, and these agency girls just aren't prepared to put up with it. They won't stay five minutes if a job proves difficult.' Mrs Harris leaned confidentially across her desk, voice lowered to reverential tones. 'And since our problem patient happens to be one of our own consultants — !

'Now I've discussed the matter with the Senior Nursing Officers and we're all in agreement that in these quite exceptional circumstances an experienced nurse of character must be assigned to help on Nazareth, with particular responsibility for Mr Galvan. It's an awful worry, you know, for Sister Carter — nurses bursting into tears and refusing to go into his room!'

'I can imagine,' murmured Christie, looking down at her neatly folded hands so that Mrs Harris shouldn't notice the twinkle in her eyes.

Tom Galvan was creating a right old pantomime, by the sound of things. Poor man! Couldn't they appreciate how frustrating it must be for him? Stuck in a hospital bed while his list built up and his neuro-surgical firm struggled to carry on as best they could without their boss man?

Experienced nurse of character indeed! The CNO was obviously afraid Christie would be wise as her surname and refuse the transfer: but at least she'd had the decency to make her proposition fair and straight.

And now she wants my answer,

thought Christie wryly. I can't let her down. She's my boss and I respect her. I don't see myself as a tough no-nonsense cookie — and I don't really think Mrs Harris does either, but she knows I've experienced worse things in life than getting bawled out by a big bully of a man. So. Might as well look dry-eyed and confident and say Wisdom is willing.

* * *

'It's going to be a question of helping Mr Galvan come to terms with what has happened. The medical staff are extremely concerned for his future, but the prognosis is hopeful.' Relief brought a cheerful smile to the CNO's face. 'It's a case, Nurse Wisdom, of *festina lente* and all shall be well.'

On this her first morning, pulling over her head the white uniform dress worn on the private wing, Christie remembered those words with foreboding. Too late now for second thoughts, nevertheless she was wondering if she might not have been foolishly rash. Private patients expected *doctors* to dance attendance upon them, even to the extent of removing their stitches. Glorified waitressing, that's what nursing would be on Nazareth Wing. Would she never get back to a medical ward?

Slender fingers snapped the press-stud fastenings in place and Christie pulled a face at her reflection in the wardrobe mirror. The dresses were a size too generous, but it had seemed sensible to make do rather than ask for a proper fitting. After all, this would be a short assignment — a couple of weeks at most.

'And one thing I shall be able to do — scotch all those scaremongering rumours that some people — who ought to know better! — have been spreading about Mr Galvan's condition.'

As she pinned up her hair into its working-day style, Christie's inward eye was dwelling on the vision of a tall impressive figure, silently smoking by his car on that fateful night. Neither of them had known what was to happen, how they would be linked together that evening, he the patient, she the nurse. Even in the dusk, when they could barely see each other, his physical presence had drawn her like a magnet into his path . . .

Suddenly aware of this ridiculous introspection, Christie jabbed a long pin punishingly into the thick twist of hair. 'Must be that novel you were reading last night in bed! Foolish romantic nonsense. Stick to the *Nursing Times* in future, Wisdom, if you want to live up to your illustrious surname.

'Oh, and *don't go falling for Galvan* like all the rest of them. You're a lucky girl to have a decent reliable boy-friend like James.

'And fingers crossed! he's on the verge of proposing.'

★ ★ ★

A path of stepping stones dotted the ribbon of lawn leading down to a brick-built garage tacked on to the bottom of Christie's tiny garden. It was damp and the stones were greasy, so she picked her way with care. To twist an ankle today of all days would be positively sickening . . .

* * *

The Sister-in-Charge concluded her brisk medical resumé of the cases on Corridor B. 'I think that's everything. If you find yourself with a quiet moment take a look at the relevant case notes. But your prime responsibility is to nurse Mr Galvan.'

'Of course, Sister.' Christie tucked notebook and pencil back into her pocket, returning the senior nurse's encouraging smile with a confidence Carol Carter was mighty relieved to perceive.

Her experienced eye liked the look of the tall, straight-backed staff nurse. No make-up. Not a hair out of place. A steady gaze that accepted her perusal without flinching. And a resolute chin above that lovely long neck.

Stamina, and a natural authority that did not offend others, according to Mrs Harris; newly qualified, but not relying on the easy option. It would take more than a frustrated surgeon to make *this* one cry. Carol Carter was getting exasperated with agency nurses bursting into tears all over the place.

Christie had made herself voice the question. Was there a possibility Mr Galvan might have suffered brain damage? People were saying . . .

Sister Carter snorted inelegantly. 'He's a naughty boy, dear, that's all — upsetting my nurses, angry with everyone and everything. Never had a day's illness before in his life — and suddenly finds he's as vulnerable as the next man!'

Her impressive bosom heaved under the expanse of dark blue cloth; but her indignation was simulated, for like all the rest Sister Carter was under the charismatic surgeon's spell.

All it needed was a nurse capable of keeping cool under fire. He was a darling, really. 'You have my permission to bind and gag him if need be! Stand up to our Tom, give him what for. I've told him he needs his bottom smacked and that the *last* person I'm sending him is a blonde student nurse with enormous . . . ' Sister Carter rolled her eyes to indicate the impossibility of the man.

Christie pulled a face in commiseration. Then her lips twitched as a sudden idea caught her imagination. It would only take a couple of minutes. And it would certainly serve him right. From all the evidence it was becoming clear that Tom Galvan was going to be the most awful patient she'd ever nursed — if she didn't take immediate steps to get the upper hand.

The telephone shrilled, and Christie took Sister's encouraging nod of dismissal to mean she should now head on up the stairs to the nurses' station on Corridor B.

And sure enough, she arrived just in time to hear an almighty racket coming from Room 27!

Prepared though she was, the shock of it still had Christie gasping in outrage. This was supposed to be a hospital, not a bear garden!

It sounded mighty like Tom Galvan had hurled his breakfast tray at someone. And the way he was bawling about the coffee — well! it was a wonder the other occupants of Corridor B didn't justifiably complain!

The staff cloakroom lay immediately to her left, so Christie with beating heart slipped inside. This was going to be a real challenge. But Dr Galvan needn't think he was going to scare the pants off his latest nurse, oh no!

Wanted to be specialled by a plumply gorgeous blonde, did he? Well, he was going the wrong way about it. Bad behaviour got its just reward.

Adding a touch of powder to her already

pale complexion, Nurse Wisdom assumed an expression of tight-lipped severity . . . yes, that looked nice and formidable! And, to complete the effect, she stuck on her nose the dark-framed reading glasses she no longer needed for close work.

Nice, old-fashioned frames, the lenses not exactly helpful for normal duties. But first impressions counted, and if the prospect of being ministered to by a no-nonsense, humourless young woman failed to bring this irascible patient to heel — then Staff Nurse Wisdom was prepared to eat her dainty white cap!

With the belt loosened, disguising her enviable waist, Christie's uniform dress hung limp as a sack. She looked suitably unappealing, if the small square mirror was anything to go by.

'You'll not overawe *me*, Mr Tom Galvan. My brief is to persuade you to be a good boy and not upset your nurses. You must learn to be a *patient* patient, and allow your body to heal in the fullness of time. And I regard it as a privilege to have been given the chance to nurse you back to health and strength. Yes, indeed!

'Might be as well if I hide this,' she added thoughtfully, unfastening her name badge and slipping it into her pocket.

There was a poor little nurse weeping on the landing, a small slip of a thing; just married, she spluttered into Christie's sympathetic ear, and trying to raise a mortgage by working for a nursing agency who paid hourly rates that seemed to a struggling young couple nothing short of wondrous. She showed the new staff nurse her ruined uniform and was comforted by the other's evident indignation.

Prudently allowing time for the surgeon to cool down, Christie decided her first priority should be to check out this unfamiliar territory. 'How odd,' she said to herself, feeling like Alice in Wonderland, 'to be walking about on carpets in my duty shoes. And all this mirror on the walls — and all those potted palms! Very 'Grand Hotel' . . . '

The greenery was shiny and dust-free. In spite of herself, Christie was impressed. The whole wing had of course been refurbished at vast expense by the private hospital group which — after much deliberation — St Joseph's administrators had brought in to manage its NHS pay beds.

'I remember,' mused Christie, 'there was a lot of contention over that decision. But I wasn't much interested at the time because I didn't see myself ever working here. Some were dead against bringing in the private sector to run our pay beds.'

Half expecting to find a sluice packed with undreamed-of space-age equipment, she was relieved to find the only thing she was going to have to get used to — rapidly! — was how to manage practical nursing wearing reading specs.

Frames lowered halfway down her nose, Christie eyed the kitchen doubtfully. Nurses were clearly expected to muscle in *here*, judging by the coffee machine bubbling away on the side and the microwave and gas hob. Heavens, if she'd wanted to be a waitress she wouldn't have wasted three years on RGN training!

No sign of a domestic — they must have cleaned earlier or be working on another corridor.

A nurse emerged briefly from Room 30 but scuttled into 29 without so much as a glance behind her, as if afraid of getting mixed up in someone else's problem. Christie's pleasant 'Hello' wafted on empty air.

'I never even had time to say cheerio to Simon and Mike and the rest of the team,' she realised regretfully, feeling very much the stranger yet again after settling down on Casualty. 'Ah well, time to beard the lion in den 27. He should have cooled off by now. And if the man's got any decency he'll be regretting that unkind carry-on.'

Yes, decided Christie, strangely reluctant after her earlier eagerness to renew acquaintance with Tom Galvan; squinting out of the window to see if it was possible to get a glimpse of the path, labs where James would be working. Yes, I bet if I walked in there without knocking, caught him by surprise with his defences down . . . There he'd be, sitting by the window in his dressing gown, a rug over his knees, his features wan and drawn, the scars on his handsome face vivid against the pallor. Drumming restless fingers on the chair arms and hating himself — the anguish in his eyes as he turns towards my unexpected entrance would be evidence of that. Why am I behaving like this? he'd plead silently. Somebody — help me. And in answer I'd whisper, here I —

Another nurse bustled past brandishing a bedpan. 'You got No. 27? — and the best of British!' she hissed, grimacing from the door of the sluice.

Christie's stomach did a swallow dive. *Courage, mon brave!* Remember this is in a *very* good cause . . .

Shoulders were squared, spectacles jabbed into place with a determined forefinger. Ashen features adopted the now-we're-going-to-behave-ourselves-aren't-we expression perfected five minutes ago in the loo.

'Enough of this prevarication,' she declaimed to the deserted corridor. 'Ten minutes ago, Christie Wisdom, you were confident enough to fight dragons bare-handed. What you have in there is a sick man who needs you. So *in* you go.'

She hardened her eye, knocked peremptorily, and before her nerve could go AWOL launched herself over the threshold of Room 27 — stepping squelch on to a soft-fried egg, which had landed sunny side up.

The man in the bed grinned.

A medical textbook with a broken spine lay on the carpet alongside a rasher of bacon. Shards of china crunched beneath her sturdy laced shoes. 'Ugh!' exclaimed Christie, hopping on one leg while twisting to examine congealed yellow yolk embedded in her ridged crêpe sole.

'Feel free to use my bathroom,' suggested the man in the bed, making no attempt to conceal his amusement, 'you're the funniest sight I've seen all week.' His left arm was out of action, being encased in plaster of Paris. With the Biro in his right hand he gestured towards an open door to starboard.

Intent on avoiding stamping yolk into the nice green carpet, Christie said nothing but slipped off her shoe and on obedient stockinged feet hurried into the bathroom to wipe her shoe clean.

Cheek! she thought, eyeing her VIP patient sidelong through the half-open bathroom door, annoyed with herself for making such a ridiculous entrance.

The VIP patient lay propped up against several pillows, apparently naked apart from his bandages. He seemed to have forgotten she was there.

The blue coverlet was littered with official-looking forms closely covered with handwriting. Mr Galvan appeared to be studying them one by one with the utmost concentration and scribbling notes on a clip-board with his uninjured right hand.

He didn't look in the least bit sorry. For himself, his behaviour — or anyone else, for that matter!

This was a considerable anticlimax, for Christie had psyched herself up to cope with . . . anything. She even felt vaguely disappointed. For far from being dismayed by her unprepossessing appearance, Mr Galvan hadn't even given her a second glance — let alone demonstrated any inclination to eat her alive — so intent was he on his papers.

Under cover of clearing up the mess of that spilled breakfast tray, she watched him with darting glances which resolved into blatant stares as Tom Galvan continued to be oblivious to her presence. He looked rested, yet there was a tension about him. And the lines scored between nose and mouth bore testimony to recent trauma. The facial cuts and grazes were now little more than fading scars. A sterile dressing protected the abdominal incision which was healing well, according to Sister Carter. But that rigid snowy plaster clearly hampered Tom Galvan's actions and irritated him. The left hand, noted Christie on automatic professional pilot, remained swollen.

It was high time this patient was out of bed and into his dressing gown. He should be encouraged to walk up and down the corridors for exercise. No one ought to be bothering him with paperwork at this early stage of recovery.

Depositing the debris in the kitchen and collecting cleaning materials from the sluice, she hurried back to mop up the carpet and complete her scrutiny to her own satisfaction.

In spite of the plaster and bandages Tom Galvan's body looked as tough and tautly-muscled as when she had prepared him for surgery. And surely no one with a serious head injury could work with such concentration?

Her brown eyes shone with relief as she wrung out the floor cloth and dropped it back into the red plastic bucket. The day would certainly come when Mr Galvan would be back in theatre healing stricken brains and saving lives.

But he'd no business lying in bed all day. Did he want to end up with a thrombosis? And what if Sir Frank should arrive for his morning's round and discover his celebrated patient in such disarray?

Whoops! In her haste Christie almost collided with the sluice door. Drat the eyewear. But she'd better maintain her angel-in-disguise appearance, for the next few days would be critical in establishing a suitably professional relationship between nurse and difficult doctor-patient.

She turned back into the corridor just in time — too late! — to see Sir Frank himself entering Tom Galvan's room. Sister Carter was with him, clasping the folder of patients' notes to her ample bosom and indicating with a flap of her free hand that she would accompany the consultant and leave Nurse Wisdom free to help with other patients.

It was over an hour before she got back to Room 27. Mr Galvan was still in bed, still studying the mass of papers which had now been stacked into several piles over locker and bed table.

Christie regarded him with appreciation. A lock of thickly curling black hair looped itself appealingly over his left eyebrow. The whiteness of linen sheets deepened the warm, smooth olive tones of his skin, the glossy tangle of hair curling over and around the sterile dressing emphasising his powerful masculinity.

No pyjamas. And no getting away from it, here was a disturbingly attractive hunk of man.

She gave a sudden start of alarm as she realised she'd been caught momentarily off her guard. Those heavy eyelids

had deceived her, dangerously concealing the direction of Tom Galvan's gaze.
But it was clear now from the way his
lips quirked in wryly amused recogni-
tion that the deepset eyes were
scrutinising this latest offering from
Carol Carter's fold of sacrificial lambs:
the bright spark who'd entertained him
earlier with her impromptu breakfast
cabaret.

Christie blushed like a teenager.
Helplessly she felt the beat of colour
transform her smooth pale cheeks.

Tom's practised eyes worked upward
from the elegant ankles. Pity they didn't
wear black stockings on Nazareth Wing.
Her hospital badge told him this was a
homegrown St Joseph's staff nurse. Bit
of a streak of lightning, she was, and so
shapeless it was hard to tell if she was
going or coming.

Hah! She'd forgotten those hideous
spectacles she could scarcely see through
. . . that blush almost made her pretty.
Wide sparkly brown eyes — at the moment
somewhat alarmed (wait till he gave her

something to be alarmed *about*!). Finely-boned slightly aquiline nose which added to her elegant aura. Firm chin. Painful-looking hairdo. And a gentle, shapely mouth that had an extraordinary tendency to turn itself into a sprung trap.

Strange lady! Tom grinned, an ironic slash of white momentarily altering his face from mature man to boy.

Falling in love on the instant had never featured on Christie's list of possibilities. Life just wasn't like that. What she was feeling now was simply the aftermath of her deep concern that so valuable a life should not be lost. Here was a man she'd witnessed on the point of death. It was impossible to keep her feelings entirely disguised.

Another of them, sighed Tom to himself. Why do they let themselves? Haven't they any pride? What is it about being a neuro-surgeon that makes a fellow damn nigh irresistible? To them all . . . except Diana.

Christie pulled herself together with an effort. The blush faded. She resumed her tough, severe disguise.

Tom wanted to laugh. So this was Carol Carter's response! Sending up a young dragon-in-training. What an anaemic creature! Pale now as a pint of milk and just as shapely.

He'd only been pulling Carol Carter's leg. Fancy her taking him *that* seriously!

'What are you doing in bed, Mr Galvan?' snapped Christie, grabbing the initiative to show the quality of her mettle. 'You should be up and in your dressing gown. Haven't you any pyjamas? Oh yes, I see you have.' She advanced purposefully and grasped a burgundy-colour sleeve protruding from beneath the heap of pillows.

'Now please put these on. And where are the bottoms?' She whisked the sheets back and peered at his legs. 'Oh, you *are* wearing them — good. Now let's get your dressing gown from behind the bathroom door and we'll have you out of bed and in that chair by the window in no time. You'll feel much better. And I can change your sheets and have the bed all nice and tidy in readiness for your afternoon nap.'

He was making not the slightest effort to insert his good arm into the right sleeve. So much for the nanny approach, thought Christie with an inward sigh. In the end she had to grab the pen from him and put it out of reach. 'Lean forward, please.' He smelled of warm sheets and shaving soap, and his body was solid and real beneath her capable hands. With ill-concealed impatience he tolerated having the jacket smoothed across his back and fastened with a safety pin across that injured arm.

Christie handed him back the pen. So far so good. He hadn't made a murmur. 'Have you had a proper bath yet? Well, we'll see about that tomorrow. You certainly haven't used a brush and comb today.' She delved inside his locker and came up with a pair of silver-backed bristle brushes. 'Here you are. Give your hair a brush. Unless you'd like me to do it for you?'

This roused him. 'Look here, Staff Nurse whoever you are, in case you are unaware of the fact, I am a doctor. I do not need you. I do not need any nurse. I can dose myself with my medicines. I can remove my own stitches. I can even record my own TPR and BP on the charts and anything else you care to name. I've told Carol Carter not to waste her precious nurses on me. There's only one thing *you* can do to please me and that is . . . get the hell out of here!'

Christie tried not to flinch in the face of this stinging attack. Feelings of hurt and affront threatened to overwhelm her, but she stamped them down out of sheer determination to stand her ground and not meet temper with temper. 'Shout at me all you wish, Mr Galvan. I promise I shan't take offence. You need to get all this fury out of your system.'

Tom swept the silver brushes through his hair and tossed them into her hands. He responded in tones of deep sarcasm: 'An amateur psychologist!' His lip curled in derision.

No, I'm not going to run away from you, Christie promised silently. Much as I might prefer to! 'I understand why you're feeling so angry and frustrated, and believe me, I truly want to help you.'

Mr Galvan's splendid teeth bared themselves in a snarl that dared Christie to continue with this impertinent declaration of empathy. A mere nurse claiming to understand what he, a neuro-surgeon, was going through, cooped up in this cell of a room when over in the theatre block his team were operating without him. Damn the accident, damn Diana, damn the whole lot of them — including the anxious creature regarding him with wide-eyed concern. If he'd stayed at the flat as planned this nightmare would never have happened. But his flat keys were back at the Manor. There'd been nothing for it but to drive wearily on to the motorway . . .

There was a knock on the door and an auxiliary came in with the elevenses tray which she handed over to Mr Galvan's poor nurse. He looked tidier than she'd seen him all week, but the new lass looked drained already. She'd last no longer than the others. Still, she'd got him into pyjamas, and that must have taken some nerve.

Because of the papers stacked over every surface there was nowhere to set the tray within Mr Galvan's reach. Christie poured his coffee and set it over near the comfortable chair by the window. No sugar. Well, that was good. 'Please get up, Mr Galvan. You know you shouldn't lie in bed too long after an operation.'

'You don't suppose I choose to be an invalid?' came the grumpy response. 'I have been getting up. But it happens to be more convenient to spread these application forms across the bed.'

'Oh, is that what they are?' Christie

fetched his tartan Scotch House dressing gown and turned back the covers for him to swing his legs out. He complied, but groaned as if it was all an immense effort. 'The light's much better here by the window, and I can pass you your papers as and when you need them.' She took hold of his good arm in case he should be unsteady on his feet. It was a shock to be reminded how tall he was, towering over her, physically dominating the confined space. No wonder the agency nurses had been frightened of Tom Galvan in rage! Herself a tall girl, Christie felt dwarfed and fragile beside him. She was taken aback when the grumbling suddenly ceased and tightening his dressing gown cord Tom looked down at her and grinned. She smiled back uncertainly, mistrusting her instinctive reaction to be charmed by this extremely attractive man.

'What's your name, nursie?'

Nursie. Christie. 'Gertie,' blabbered

Christie, the first name that sprung to mind.

'You look a darn sight better without your goggles, Gertie. You seem to see a lot better without them too.'

Drat! She'd taken them off to help out with bed-making — and forgotten to resume her disguise. 'Oh, I — er — sometimes use them for reading case notes or writing up reports. I took them off to do the beds. Now I'll just see to yours, if you're sure you're quite comfortable here. Which pile of forms would you like to start with?'

Five minutes passed in which Christie bustled back and forth with fresh linen and Tom Galvan resumed his work.

'Coffee okay, Mr Galvan? Another cup?'

He flung down his pen with a sigh. 'I trained myself to be ambidextrous — always useful for a surgeon. But my right hand's not used to this and I'm getting writer's cramp.'

'Perhaps I could help you.'

'Hmm. This is strictly confidential. I can't allow you to read the applications.' Tom rubbed his chin slowly, considering this useful offer of assistance. He could wait for his secretary to come up in the late afternoon. On the other hand, here was this obviously intelligent young woman offering her services . . .

'I guess you could help me draw up my shortlist.'

Christie brought across a wooden chair and settled herself alertly at his elbow with the clipboard.

'Put your goggles on, Gertie.'

'Wha-? Ah, right!' She fished in her pocket with a pretence of brisk necessity, beginning to regret having turned herself into such a fright.

'These are applications for the post of SHO on my neuro-surgical firm,' Mr Galvan explained. 'I need a shortlist of ten names.'

Christie sounded incredulous. '*All* these? But there must be over a hundred!'

He gave a grunt. 'We've had a high response to our advert — and my secretary has already weeded out the no-hopes. Every one of these doctors has excellent qualifications. Blame the cutbacks. Poor wretches! I hate rejecting good men.'

'And good women,' said Christie firmly.

'Quite.'

Her eyes challenged his. 'So there will be five female surgeons on your shortlist?'

'Not likely, Gertie! A good woman's hard to find.'

★   ★   ★

'So how was it, your first experience of Nazareth and the wicked Tom Galvan?'

James's uncharacteristic facetiousness surprised Christie. They were sitting together in the canteen having a cup of tea before she departed homeward. James kept glancing at his watch. He had set up a controlled test in the lab — part of his research — and half an hour was as much as he could allow himself for a snack of beans on toast and a shared pot of tea with Christie, who had just come off duty.

'Well, this morning wasn't so bad, but it's ridiculous the number of people who kept trooping in throughout the afternoon. Mr Galvan's senior regis-trar — '

'Kingsley Armstrong?'

'Yes, Kingsley, that's right. Well, he came and stayed *ages* going over theatre lists and discussing patients. And Mr Galvan's secretary — she seemed very young, Cecilia's her name — brought across letters to sign and he told her to be back to take dictation first thing in the morning. Plus half the senior medical staff fobbing me off with beaming smiles and 'Just going to put my head round the door and say hello'. Doctors disturbing him — another cup, James dear? — who should know better. Mr Galvan got no rest to speak of. And as for the flowers! These gorgeous bouquets keep arriving and he just says oh, have them sent over to the wards, I don't want this torture chamber turned into a mausoleum.'

She prattled on, and James listened with half an ear now that he'd satisfied himself Christie had ended her first day unscathed. He was preoccupied with the complex reactions taking place at that very moment on his lab bench. 'What it is to be popular and loved by all,' sighed Christie. 'That television doctor, Diana Diamond, sent two dozen red roses. Red roses to a man!' She paused for a second or two's reflection. 'Mr Galvan kept *those* in his room. He seemed happier, after they came. Quieter, more settled. I wonder why that was?'

James looked up in surprise. Then his brow cleared. Of course, it must have been before Christie came to St Joseph's. 'Those two were engaged once upon a time. For all I know they still are. She was a medical SHO at King's. I used to see her around Joe's when she came down to stay with Galvan. That was before she got snaffled up by the BBC to present that TV programme *Best of Health*. Very striking lady.'

'I think she's beautiful,' said Christie quietly, cradling her cup in both hands, conjuring up from memory the glamorous screen image of Diana Diamond.

'A knockout — extremely sexy. But not beautiful. *You* are beautiful, Christie.' James was glancing at his watch as he spoke, pushing back his chair. Christie rose too, following him out of the canteen, grasping at his sleeve.

'And am *I* sexy, James?' she questioned breathlessly, fully expecting him to say yes, pet, of course you are.

James eyed her up and down and he wasn't smiling. His mind was already at work on more serious matters. 'Heavens, no, sweetheart,' he said kindly, believing that this reassuring answer was just what a dear, sensible girl like Christie Wisdom longed to hear. 'Have you been going round like that all day with your belt not properly fastened?'

'Grrr!' sulked a very confused staff nurse, heading home to her single bed.

4

Christie withdrew the needle of a hypodermic containing 20 mls of blood and pressed cotton wool to the punctured vein in the crook of Tom's right elbow. Automatically Tom folded his arm, answering her encouraging smile with a baleful, if evidently relieved, scowl as he relaxed back into his pile of pillows. 'Now,' suggested Christie brightly to her very awkward patient, 'repeat after me, 'Thank you very much, Staff, that was really perfectly tolerable'.'

Tom emitted a sound somewhere between a growl and a sneer. He was to remain in bed till the doctor arrived to examine him.

Concealing a sigh, Christie printed the necessary details on the red-labelled sterile specimen container. She was rapidly coming to the conclusion that the only way to deal with Tom Galvan was to tell him in a firm tone of voice what she was about to do — and then get on with the job before he had time to start an argument. That complicated fracture of the humerus (which the orthopods were keeping under strict surveillance) somewhat cramped his style.

I know it's rotten of me, she reflected wryly, but an armful of plaster does render him marginally easier to manage!

On Room 27's record card Christie began filling in details of all drugs, treatments and sterile disposables used that morning. Everything, down to the last pre-injection Medi-Swab, must be accounted for. Not that there'd be a bill at the end of the day for Nazareth's most cherished patient.

As she worked she kept a discreet eye upon the injured surgeon, studying his aloof and brooding profile. It didn't take much imagination to guess what was on his mind.

According to the records he'd be thirty-four next birthday. Christie's blue Biro hovered in mid-air. In his early twenties Tom must have been handsome as a Greek god. Maturity had bruised the youthful perfection and added an amiable cynicism to his manner. All this plus the high-octane intelligence which was the hallmark of a neuro-surgeon, and the aura of power surrounding any highly qualified and experienced man, whatever his profession.

Obviously in no hurry to tether himself to that television girl-friend, mused Christie in something of a daydream. She chewed the end of her pen meditatively. And after the Wisdom saga I can't say I blame him. If I hadn't had the good fortune to meet my steady reliable James, wild horses wouldn't have dragged *me* to the altar. She looked at what she had written and before she could stop herself laughed aloud.

'What's the matter with you?' growled

Tom Galvan, sounding like a bear with a sore head.

'I've just written 'Nazareth Wing, Cage 27' instead of Room 27! Whatever can I have been thinking of?' Christie clapped a hand across her mouth and rocked with ill-advised mirth.

'Very funny. So what does that make me, huh?'

'How about a wounded panther?' hiccuped his nurse through her giggles.

'And you're the panther-tamer?' suggested Tom with ominous silkiness, plotting narrow-eyed revenge. Christie read his expression and her laughter caught in her throat . . .

At this opportune moment the door opened and in strolled Sir Frank, accompanied by Jonathan Reeves, the senior orthopaedic consultant, Sister Carter on their heels. Christie's back was turned as she bent over her trolley.

'Morning, Tom. Morning, Staff. Aha! I see the TLC I wrote you up for is already proving effective.' He turned to his companions, arms spread wide in a gesture that embraced the room. 'We're looking at the *old* Tom, kempt and cared for. Congratulations, Christie Wisdom! we knew you were the lass for the job. Tender Loving Care — never fails to revitalise a good man.'

He beamed at Christie, who was stifling a nervous giggle at this unwitting revelation of her true identity. Tender loving care indeed! A sockful of lead on the back of the head would be a more appropriate prescription for this restless, ungrateful, disobedient patient.

Her fingers located the plastic name badge tucked away and forgotten in her pocket. Might as well pin that back on her chest and flex her nerve for the high jump!

'So *this*,' drawled the dapper Mr Reeves, 'is the alert young woman who saved you from haemorrhaging to death, dear boy. It's not easy to put gratitude into words, but I know you'll have done your best. And the same goes for us all.' Jonathan Reeves was in his late forties and famous for his sharp taste in suits. He was privately thinking that he'd never seen such a spectacular waistline on a nurse: surely eighteen inches went out with the Victorians? No wonder Tom was perking up at last, with that hourglass shape flittering round him all day!

Christie had been mortified by James's comment; she'd not meant to leave Nazareth looking so peculiar, but her preoccupation with her patient had driven superficial considerations right out of mind. This morning she was her everyday self — not that Tom Galvan had commented on any improvement.

It was no longer possible to continue this pretence of setting the dressings trolley to rights. Nothing for it but to face the consultants and bite the inside of her lip in a flush of embarrassment. Such exaggeration! And in front of Mr Galvan too! A calm sort of protest was out of the question. 'I — I didn't . . . it wasn't . . . anyone would have . . . '

But no one was listening.

'Been behaving himself, then, has he, Staff?'

Christie's eye was baleful as she handed over the blue vinyl folder which contained the TPR charts, drug prescription and administration records, and X-ray request forms. She murmured something noncommittal, for it would be evident from the nursing records, at any rate, that the patient was making satisfactory progress.

'Pulse is seventy-six a minute. Blood pressure a hundred and thirty over eighty. Great stuff!' enthused Sir Frank as if he was reading aloud from the latest block-buster. 'Knew you'd be in good hands, Tom, with Staff here to special you.'

Sir Frank was running a shrewd professional eye over Christie herself. She was much quieter than he'd realised: even shy, or so it seemed today. If he hadn't seen the evidence with his own eyes he'd be doubting the lass was really up to such a tricky assignment. Yet somehow she seemed to be making headway with her obstinate patient. Gratitude would be smoothing her path, of course, and rightly so: not that any of them had considered this possibility when Nurse Wisdom's name was put forward.

'And nice to see *you* looking less peaky, my dear. Marks like sooty thumbprints you had under your eyes the morning after Tom's dreadful accident.' Frank himself had acquainted the neuro-surgeon with all the details surrounding his dramatic arrival at Casualty; he had certainly told of the vital part RGN Wisdom had played. 'Gave us a helluva fright, you did, boyo. It was real touch and go-o-o,' the long Welsh vowels were even more pronounced.

'So you keep reminding me,' murmured Tom, with a wry lift of an eyebrow.

Jonathan Reeves stepped over to the bed and took hold of Tom's left hand. He pinched a fingernail and viewed with satisfaction the immediate flush of pink. Christie hovered close by, ready to deal with obstructive clothing or bedding, watching and listening attentively as Mr Reeves carried out his examination.

'Mrs Macdonald has been giving you physiotherapy daily, has she not? There's no swelling of the hand now. How does your arm seem today?'

'There's not much pain.' Tom flexed and contracted muscles and tendons as the physio had instructed. His face was a mask of sheer and stubborn determination, the mouth a grim line, the eyes narrowed in concentration.

'This still comfortable?' Jonathan Reeves rapped a knuckle on the plaster cast. It gave off an odd chalky sound.

'It's a confounded nuisance,' returned his patient ungratefully. 'Look here, Jon, you've got to be straight with me. What are the possibilities? I've a fair idea of what the complications could be,' he added grimly, 'and I know I'm not out of the wood yet.'

Christie listened to the specialist with absolute concentration. She'd nipped into the School of Nursing before going home to read up in the library about complicated fractures of the humerus involving damage to adjacent structures, arteries, veins, nerves and muscles. Thrombosis was the obvious and most immediate danger to watch out for. Less serious in the upper arm because the alternative blood supply could take over if a major artery became blocked by a blood clot. In the elbow, however, such a clot could cause death of muscles of the forearm.

And there were other complications to be aware of, as Mr Reeves was explaining. Major threats to a surgeon's career . . .

Not while *I*, Christie was telling herself grimly, am nursing this patient. His life is too precious, too valuable. There will be no complications, if I have to keep them at bay by sheer force of will. I shall be here, observing and recording every detail concerning Mr Galvan's condition. And if anything does go wrong, I'll be shouting for you and Sir Frank!

' . . . with diminished or absent radial pulse, coolness and pallor of the skin of the forearm indicating the onset of arterial thrombosis.'

Christie was mentally filing every instruction concerning nursing care, an intent little frown creasing her brow.

Propped up against the pillows, Tom regarded her with interest. Young Gertie looked as if her smooth high forehead held the weight of the world and all its worries. Of course it was merely the straightforward professional concern of someone who took the nursing process and its attendant responsibilities most seriously. At first he'd suspected that true to form his new nurse was nurturing the usual fantasies about romance with a brain surgeon! But no, she was much too sweet and sensible — beneath that stern façade she liked to assume if she suspected Tom was likely to put up a fight over something. And besides, considered Tom, heavy-eyed, there was a boyfriend. Dr Mallory, none other.

Now who had passed on that gem of information? Was it Frank, suspecting Tom might enjoy the challenge of enticing this one away from her lover? Frank was not a fan of Diana's. He'd never said so, of course — much too canny for that. But there was a certain look in his eye whenever her celebrated name cropped up. And Tom could plainly read the other's mind as he poked his nose into the fading magnificence of Diana's red roses and pulled a disparaging face at their scentlessness.

Mr Reeves completed his examination and departed for his outpatients' clinic, escorted to the front door by Sister Carter, who had sent Nurse Wisdom along to her office to pin up the new off-duty list.

Sir Frank, glad of a chance to chat à deux, checked over the internal soft-tissue injuries and pronounced himself well satisfied with the healing process. Then he settled companionably in the chair by the window, still keeping a quizzical eye on the great urn of roses, ritually watered each morning by Christie when she arrived.

'I wonder if I can guess who sent those?'

'Huh,' grunted Tom discouragingly, trying to fold his arms and yet again — infuriatingly! — coming up against the rigid plaster imprisoning his left side.

'Has Diana been to see you?' Frank knew perfectly well she couldn't have. He'd received several urgent transatlantic calls, inconsiderately timed to disturb him from deepest slumber. Not that he intended to say so.

'She's in Phoenix, Arizona, making a documentary for the next series.' Tom's expression was ironic. I know she rang you, Frank, you old bastard, because she said so. 'We've spoken on the phone: says she's worried sick about me.'

Of course she is, the madam! scowled the Welshman. A brilliant and beautiful neuro-surgeon is one thing; a lame duck's quite a different kettle of fish, if you'll pardon my mixed metaphors. Sooner our Tom gets that woman out of his hair the better, and settles down with a genuine St Joseph's girl. Looks aren't that important; I've always said so. Someone kind and caring. Out loud he put the craftily attractive suggestion he'd been saving for when the moment was ripe. 'You could go home next week . . . so long as nothing untoward happens between now and then.' He examined his short and immaculate fingernails, buffed them on his chalk-striped jacket. 'You'll need some help, of course, for a few weeks till the plaster comes off.' He stared out of the window at a pale blue sky studded with a scurry of white clouds. 'Weather's picking up now. Soon be Maytime.'

Tom brightened visibly. 'What sort of help? You mean a BUPA nurse?'

'Any sort of nurse, as long as she's

not already under contract.' Frank waited for Tom to grasp the bait. 'Anyone you had in mind?'

'Not especially. Gertie's not a bad girl, though. Not much to look at, but she has a pleasant manner and gets on with the job.'

'You mean, stands no messing.'

'Eh?'

'I said efficient, but quiet with it.'

'You didn't, but I shall ignore the implication. Anyway, you couldn't possibly understand what it's like for a doctor suddenly to find himself in the rôle of patient. It's very hard to come to terms with.' A pause. 'She'll be under contract, though.'

'Temporary, I believe. She's waiting for a staff job to come up on one of the medical wards. I'll make enquiries. Don't mention anything, though, to anyone. All depends on how you seem to be over the next week. And a word of advice in your ear, boyo. *Don't* keep calling her Gertie . . . I can't imagine what started that off!'

Christie was saved from the inquisition to come by Mr Galvan's secretary, Cecilia, who was waiting outside in the corridor with her dictation pad and the morning's post. As Sir Frank walked out, Cecilia trotted in on confident stilettos. She was pert and blonde and pretty, only nineteen but with a five-star efficiency invaluable to her demanding but appreciative boss.

At the nurses' station one of the Corridor B staff was boredly flipping through the Kardex. 'You're a dark horse and no mistake,' she exclaimed, eyeing Christie's graceful approach. 'I could have sworn they'd sent a right old frump to special our Tom. All of a sudden you look quite different! Pardon my saying so, but those glasses you wear don't do a thing for you. You want some of these new fashion frames. Red would suit you a treat.'

She peered more closely. Wisdom had really lovely milky skin, and her eyes were naturally dark-lashed, large and clear. If she took a bit of trouble with herself, ditched that 'efficient nurse' hairdo and emphasised the wide-curved mouth with scarlet lipstick . . . mmm, she could do better for herself than Dullsville Dr Mallory. Might even hook her VIP patient! Well, why not? It often happened in private hospitals, grateful men patients falling hook, line and sinker for their nurses and proposing marriage and a share of worldly goods.

And it was about time Tom Galvan settled down with a wife of his own and let hundreds of fluttery hopeful hearts slow down to a normal beat!

Marriage had much to recommend it. Sarah stuck out her left hand, admiring the bright new gold band encircling her third finger. Her smile had the glow of deep satisfaction.

An elbow nudged Christie in the ribs. 'Hey up! Here comes Miss World.'

The door of Room 27 opened and closed and Cecilia trotted past with a cheery wave and a complicit wink at the nurse she reckoned had saved the day. Her skirt was tight black leather and her patent court shoes had four-inch heels.

'Trust Tom to fix himself up with a glamour girl! Better go and check his blood pressure, eh, Christie? How on earth she keeps her balance in such high heels! . . . I bet she's *tiny* without them. I can't wear any sort of heel after being in flatties all day. You should just hear my joints creak!'

'Everyone's joints creak, but only idiots listen to them,' interrupted an unsympathetic doctor who had over-heard this last complaint. 'Now what about this hysterectomy who's having trouble with her waterworks?'

'Ooh yes, my Italian lady, Mrs Graziella Carmichael. Half a mo and I'll find her notes. Here we are. Keeps moaning she can't go.'

'Is she drinking plenty?'

'What do you think, Doctor?' said the nurse cheekily, twisting a permed curl in front of her left ear.

'Right then, let's go and inform the lady that water always runs downhill.'

Christie found herself alone with a moment's peace. If Mr Galvan wanted her he'd doubtless press his buzzer. From the kitchen came the sound of Bridget, the auxiliary, singing Ave Maria as she washed the coffee cups. A bowed figure plodded past in slippers and dressing gown, the cord unfastened and dangling near the ground.

'Everything all right, Mr Rau?'

Mr Rau was a physicist from Southampton University. He'd been admitted for investigative surgery following digestive problems. Christie left her post in order to fasten the cord more securely about his lean middle. 'We don't want you tripping up and injuring yourself,' she smiled, putting a hand lightly on his stooped woollen shoulder, sensing he was trying to avoid eye contact. 'Can I help you?' she asked gently. Naturally the poor man must be feeling very anxious about his health.

'I am just walking up and down the corridor, to stretch my legs.' The black eyes trying to avoid hers were moist with fear.

Until the result of the biopsy was known there was little positive reassurance Christie could offer. When he returned to his room, though, she resolved to pop in and see whether he felt able to discuss his worries with her.

At that moment the telephone shrilled. 'Would you go to early lunch, please. They're running late over in Theatres and Nurse Maychick's gall bladder won't be back before twelve-thirty.'

'Certainly, Sister,' and there goes my counselling session with Mr Rau. Christie cupped her chin in her hand and thought for a moment. Unless I can fit something in this afternoon. Besides, I shouldn't mind at all if the wrath of Tom gets postponed till tomorrow — allowing me time to come up with an excuse for claiming to be a dragon called Gertie! Sir Frank, you have nicely dropped me in the stew!

Glancing at her fob watch, she saw

that it was time to get over to the canteen. It was unlikely she'd see James today: he tended to eat late, if at all. Especially if it meant interrupting his research project. If anyone could do with a dose of TLC it was Dr James Mallory.

What James needs is a wife, thought Christie with a decisive nod of her head; blissfully unaware that another had stood on that very spot not ten minutes earlier and matched her up with quite another man.

'Tender loving care,' she repeated with a wry smile. Oh, I know I was full of understanding and the milk of human kindness to begin with, but any man who can reduce me to such crass stupidity as giving false names and blundering about in glasses I can't see through is no candidate for being dosed with TLC by Christie Wisdom. Just what did Sir Frank Davy write on those case notes, I wonder? Perhaps a quick look . . .

And there it was, scribbled in pencil

and just waiting to be rubbed out at the first opportunity. 'TLC — to be administered according to the wisdom of Christie.' Followed by a sentence that snatched at Christie's breath and caused her shoulders to heave in agitation as she slammed the notes back into their folder . . . Not likely! not even if they fetch out the thumbscrews, not never, not nohow. No!

★ ★ ★

It was five o'clock and time to go off duty.

'You've been avoiding me, Gertie!'

'I think that's hardly fair, Mr Galvan!' Christie set her hands on her hips and compressed her lips into a thin line. Her indignation was no pretence. Not a moment's rest for her patient this afternoon. His pulse was slightly up and his deepset eyes glittered unnaturally. 'Far too many people come traipsing in and out of here. And just look at all this work your secretary's brought along

127

— I've never known anything like it! Most patients are happy to rest quietly with an interesting novel and their families visiting for an hour or so. I know full well that most of these people are coming in with problems they're expecting you to sort out for them. Talking shop instead of giving you a mental break from Joseph's.'

'Perhaps I should discharge myself?' suggested Tom slyly. 'My home is way out in the wilds, no one could bother me there and I have a housekeeper living near by.'

Christie looked worried, as well she might. How awful if her nagging should drive her patient to discharge himself! 'Sir Frank will decide when you're fit to leave Nazareth. Even then I don't see how you can possibly manage without help. That cast isn't to be taken off till June. Please, Mr Galvan, don't do anything so drastic.'

'Suddenly I feel like a bath.' With difficulty Tom struggled to his feet, stretching his spine and rotating his broad shoulders. How bitterly galling it was to find himself hampered and handicapped, with stiffening muscles and weakened limbs. A soak in piping hot water seemed just the ticket.

'What, *now*? When I'm going off duty?'

'No problem. You can post some letters for me. Just fix some of that plastic over my cast and I'll manage fine.'

He stood in front of Christie, who reached up and helped him off with his pyjama jacket. There was a heat coming off his skin that worried her. She wondered about taking his temperature again, bit her lip but concealed her anxiety; better stay and see Tom safely bathed and back in his bed.

'You must be awfully tired. Why don't I just give you a blanket bath instead?'

With one hand Tom undid his pyjama cord, let the trousers drop to the carpet and unconcernedly kicked them out of his path.

Christie picked them up, shook out the creases and laid them neatly across the bed. Clean on that morning, his pyjamas would do for another night's wear. The label inside caught her eye: High & Mighty. Her mouth curved in a wry smile. Clothes for men of heroic build. Tom was heroically built all right, and didn't he know it!

She pushed into the small bathroom where he was fiddling with the taps. That injured arm affected his balance. 'Don't you go falling over on me, will you, Mr Galvan? I couldn't possibly pick you up.'

Tom grinned down at her happily. She had a droll sense of humour, this one. He didn't feel at all tired. But it was nice to have a kind girl show some concern. And he didn't want her to go home — yet. Not before he'd had the chance to get some satisfactory answers to his questions. It suddenly occurred to him why the evenings dragged after she disappeared off to God knows where. It was like losing a companion.

He waited, magnificently naked and not one whit embarrassed, while in the cramped bathroom his nurse ran his bath, tested the water with a careful hand, set soap and towels ready and prepared to help wash him as she did most mornings.

'I shall be glad when I can do all this for myself again.'

That was a good one! Tom looked about as dissatisfied as a sultan in a harem, and Christie felt a chuckle irresistibly surfacing. This was unwise since her mouth was full of safety pins as she swathed his plaster cast in a protective layer of plastic. She didn't respond till her mouth was empty, but her shoulders heaved in silent mirth.

This didn't go unnoticed. She's laughing at me, the minx! thought Tom. Shall I tip her in the bath? On second thoughts, better not . . .

'There, that should do the trick. Now hold on to my shoulder and hop in.' She had donned a disposable apron to protect her white dress.

Several moments later came a yelp from the bath. 'Give me the flannel, Gertie — I'm not *that* helpless!'

He tipped his head to the right and sloshed water over his hair while Christie reached for the shampoo. In spite of the fresh abdominal scar and the damaged left arm Tom looked as strong as a bull. And it turned her heart over the way he grinned and said, 'We make a great team, Gertie — see, we've got our routine off to perfection — not a drop of water on the plaster today.' Then without a moment's pause and in exactly the same affable tone came the big one.

'Why didn't you tell me it was you in Casualty the night I was brought in? . . . And why on earth take off your name badge?'

Bowled at her out of the blue, his questions rocked Christie back on her heels. Her mouth opened and closed soundlessly as with alarm she saw the laughter quite gone from eyes like coals and sensed his ominously contained anger.

But he reached out a long wet arm and dabbed shampoo lather on the end of her nose. 'I'm told I should be grateful to you. And the odd thing is, I haven't remembered a thing about the accident. Till now, that is . . . '

The accident. He made it sound quite inconsequential. In silence Christie passed him a soft white bath towel. Tom was not to know it, but she'd been taking his laundry home and washing everything herself at night.

'I was — driving,' he continued slowly, 'something wrong — with my eyes. I kept seeing shadows flickering across my windscreen.' No, not shadows, images of . . . beckoning sirens?

With an unused corner of the towel Tom dabbed gently at Christie's soapy nose, thinking to himself what a delicate structure of bone and gristle and what clear pale skin she had, unmarked by even a freckle. She blinked at his touch and he realised with misgiving that she was steeling herself not to flinch. She must have believed he raised a hand to strike her!

Pain twisted his gut. Was he then so terrifying? But his brain continued its relentless search to collect the pieces of the nightmare jigsaw and fit them into place.

Neither of them spoke again till Tom was in pyjamas and tartan dressing gown. 'I'll have my supper over here,' he said, crossing to the window and staring out into the dusky evening. He seemed to have forgotten she hadn't answered his questions, so wrapped up was he in his own thoughts. Puzzled, Christie wondered what to do: whether to slip away with a quiet goodnight or get the confession over and done with. Frankly the latter choice seemed preferable.

Suddenly Tom swung round and caught her hesitating there, disposable apron in one hand, the other fiddling uncertainly with the badge which proclaimed her 'Christie Wisdom RGN'. There wasn't a trace of understanding in his manner. 'So?' he questioned with mocking arrogance, and his voice was as hard as his granite eye.

Christie looked sullen. No one would have guessed that inside she felt the most extraordinary longing to stay here all night with Tom Galvan and blow the consequences.

'I didn't tell you my name because I knew Sir Frank had — er — told you about a nurse called Christie Wisdom who was supposed to have ... well, I mean, I was only doing my job and anyone would have done the same, wouldn't they? Specially for someone like you. One of our own surgeons.'

Christie shrugged expressive shoulders and fixed her tormentor with a braver eye. Pull yourself together, gal, and give it to him straight. Tell the truth and shame the devil. 'I certainly didn't want you feeling under some kind of — well — obligation to be *nice*. It seemed far better for you to get your negative feelings out in the open air.

Explode if you wanted to.'

Tom hadn't moved a muscle; waiting for her to get on with what she was saying and clear out. 'Let's face it, you aren't exactly an ideal patient, are you!' she burst out, her cheeks flaring red with passion. 'You were getting through more nurses than I've had hot dinners. But I,' Christie jabbed herself in the chest with a shaky forefinger, 'I was foolish enough to believe I could help you come to terms with this *tragic* thing that's happened to you. I was prepared to put up with your anger and frustration in the hope that in time you'd be able to think positively about your future!'

Now who's yelling! she chided herself. Stay cool. Keep your voice calm and level. 'And so I decided to conceal my identity and pretend to be a bit strict. First I wanted you to see I was determined to stand my ground. And second I wanted to be the best possible nurse you could ever have,' she finished proudly, with stubbornly tilted chin.

Tom was rooted to the spot, fascinated by the girl's total involvement with his situation. He could see the internal play of her emotions through her transparent skin. She *identified* with what she called his tragedy. This was no crush. He didn't know what it was on her part, but he knew what it could easily become on his.

'So. If I didn't know your name — Christie Wisdom, once heard, not easily forgotten — you reckoned you'd get away with it. An angel in disguise. Pretending to be a dragon when your true reason was entirely — ' Tom had been about to say philanthropic, but at the last moment changed it mockingly to 'for love of me.'

Christie's nails ripped into the plastic apron. 'Now you're being ridiculous, Mr Galvan!' She was cold with fury. From red her face had drained white and shocked. The sardonic twist of Tom's mouth goaded her on.

'I realise you've come to take it for granted you're irresistible to women.

Perhaps I'm the first, I wouldn't know, but I do assure you *my* concern for your case is entirely and one hundred per cent professional.'

His smile lit up his darkly brooding face like a flash of light. 'What a relief! Pax it is then, Gertie. Now if you'll hand me my briefcase perhaps I can get something constructive done before they interrupt me with supper.'

★   ★   ★

It wasn't until she had changed and was about to leave the building that Christie remembered Tom's letters. She was over an hour late: not that there was anyone or anything to rush home for. And the letters might be important. But why should she give up more of her own time to run errands for such an ungrateful and arrogant man? Why indeed?

She hesitated at the foot of the stairs. It wouldn't take a minute just to run up and fetch them. If she didn't he'd assume she was sulking. Which I most certainly am, Christie reminded herself indignantly. Informing me I was in *love* with him. He may be an expert on brains, but he knows next to nothing about hearts!

She pressed a hand against the thumping of her own heart. It had started up again the moment she considered going back up to Room 27.

Wisdom! warned the voice of conscience, watch your step! You've got all the symptoms of a pythonic crush on Tom Galvan.

Christie bit her lip and sighed. I'm afraid your diagnosis is correct. I have to confess it's like wrestling with a demon snake to keep my feelings under control when I'm close to him. But don't worry, conscience, it's purely a physical thing. I love James. I want to marry James and cook his meals and wash his socks, and *that's* what love is all about. I think . . .

'Hello, Christie! Didn't know you were on a late today.' A cloaked and capped figure was regarding Christie curiously as she dithered by the stairs. 'Forgot something!' was the breathless explanation, and Christie disappeared in a scramble of long legs and flying loose hair. Outside Tom Galvan's door she took a deep breath and knocked. Then assuming her usual cool and composed persona she stepped back into the lion's den.

★　★　★

For once Tom's concentration was letting him down. He tipped his papers on to the bed and from a packet secreted on the top shelf of the fitted wardrobe found and lit a small cigar. He smoked very little; but on Nazareth it was totally verboten.

One cigarillo to increase brain arousal.

Tom was making little headway with the photocopy he'd been sent of Dr Engelun's paper on the pineal gland. Engelun was an eminent German neurologist and his paper too hot off the press to have been translated. Besides, without a dictionary the effort was pretty useless. Tom knew his scant German wasn't up to the task.

Anyway, his mind was preoccupied with Nurse Wisdom to a most extraordinary degree. What in hell was the matter with him? Wisdom. Wisdom. Wisdom . . . Wisdom's the angelic face floating over him when he thought he was dying. Wisdom's the voice that had whispered reassurance in his ear. Wisdom's the cool hand on his forehead as the pain in his right side increased to an unbelievable agony.

Memory was coming back to him now, details triggering each other off as they surfaced in his brain . . . a chill sweat broke out on Tom's brow as mentally he relived through the horror and the pain.

Trapped alone in the wreckage of the Porsche, he'd known there were grave internal injuries. And something was disastrously wrong with his left arm.

With his hand raised he could feel a radial pulse which disappeared when the hand was lowered. The main bone in his arm — the humerus, he gauged to be splintered. And all it needed was one sliver of shattered bone to spear the main artery and render his operating hand withered and useless for ever. He must not lose consciousness. He must hold that arm rigid and immovable against his injured torso.

Wisdom, living up to her surname, had sensed the intensity of his will and allowed no one to interfere till expert help arrived on the scene. And she was the one who had brought Frank to him just in the nick of time.

Yes, there was everything to be grateful for. And some day . . .

Tom exhaled gustily out of the opened window and at the same time cursed the day he'd been reduced to behaving like a naughty schoolboy, his freedom and privacy so monstrously curtailed.

A knock interrupted his reverie. His

room door opened. He turned angrily at this unwelcome intrusion . . .

To confront the missing link, the one piece of the jigsaw which till now had refused to fall into place.

5

'You!'

'Mr Galvan — ' began Christie. Electricity sparked the atmosphere, freezing the admonition hovering on her lips.

Tom slowly raised the thin cigar and drew a long, deliberate inhalation. Behind the camouflage of smoke his face remained inscrutable; but everything was clicking into place. 'I knew there was something special about you, Nurse Wisdom; something I couldn't put my finger on . . . ' he murmured into the veil of smoke that hung between them.

This night Tom was learning a great deal about the events which had almost cost him his life — and might yet have ruined his career. And now in front of him stood the flesh-and-blood reality of someone he'd believed to be no more than an insubstantial trick of the imagination — an illusion, a tantalising dream.

There *had* been a girl in a car park. And she was none other than the off-duty version of Gertie! What, mused Tom, his face a bitter mask, would be her reaction when Wisdom learned that it was she herself who had sent the Porsche spinning out of control?

All along he'd been convinced that in spite of their theories he'd not fallen asleep at the wheel. He, Tom Galvan, master of steely concentration in the operating theatre, schooled to ignore physical discomfort on the precarious tightrope of brain surgery. Was it likely he'd be careless at the wheel of a high-performance sports car?

It was all coming back to him now, his close and silent observation of the mermaid creature locking up her car and walking — apparently — straight into his arms. Graceful and loose-limbed, the fantasy of her had lived on vividly in his imagination: immensely appealing after Diana's contrived and artificial glamour.

Why, no doubt about it, Nurse Wisdom might have saved his life — but she'd damn near finished him off in the first place!

'I came back because I forgot the letters you wanted me to post. And here you are smoking when you know perfectly well — '

In two strides Tom was confronting her, the glowing point of his cigar stabbing at her emphatically, mere inches from Christie's startled nose. She pressed back against the door, dry-throated with uncertainty, her fingers spread helplessly against the solid barrier of wood.

'You forget, young woman, that I myself am a doctor and fully in control of my faculties. This one solitary cigar has a positive contribution to make *at this moment* to my well-being. And let me tell you, I have fingertip control over every single thing I do in this life. Which at the moment, Gertie, you would do well to be thankful for!'

Tom would have grabbed the girl and chucked her bodily on to the bed while he blocked her retreat and forced her to help him finish this horrendous mental jigsaw. But his disabled arm prevented such a desirable course of action. So, taking his time over it, he leaned back against the windowsill and enjoyed this illicit smoke.

The brooding melancholy of his eyes was almost unbearable. In mute confusion Christie waited: not moving an inch, her spine pressed rigid against the door. Why didn't I get away while the going was good! she agonised. Why do I give in to these Girl Guide impulses? I could be . . . I could be the other side of the shopping centre by now. I could be putting the car away, unlocking the front door, safe inside, I could be . . .

Her forlorn expression began to penetrate Tom's self-absorbed mood. He hadn't been seeing Staff Nurse Wisdom in mufti. This was the girl from his dreams in her tight black velvet jeans and loosely enveloping black sweater, that waterfall of shining dark brown hair falling smoothly from the high pale forehead to halfway down her narrow back. An uncomplicated girl with a face innocent of artifice, huge wounded eyes staring anxiously up into his.

What Christie was seeing was part of the very same photograph etched into her memory: Tom, in the dusky night, brooding and masterful and compellingly attractive. Whole and unharmed as he prepared to drive off into the darkness.

It was impossible, of course. But more than anything she wanted to reach out and put her arms round him and comfort him. Through sheer force of will press back time to the days before the accident, when Tom was his old confident outgoing self, blessed with good fortune, good health and brute strength.

A time, she recognised sadly, when you didn't even know I existed.

How her fingers ached to stroke his tousled black hair, still wet from the bath. It needed cutting and curled about his neck and ears in a way that in ordinary circumstances he'd never have tolerated. At his temples glinted a sprinkling of silver which with a little catch of breath Christie realised she hadn't noticed before. Was it the accident? Severe trauma could turn people's hair white. Had she misunderstood — had they *all* misunderstood the depths of despair and misery to which Tom's crippling injuries had reduced him?

How could I have been so unkind as to reproach him over one miserable cigar? she accused herself.

There were shadows beneath his eyes and a vein pulsed rhythmically in his temple. The sense of ominously cooped-up energy throbbed and vibrated upon the atmosphere. Tensely Christie watched and waited for something — anything! — to happen . . .

Tom coughed. He realised that his

chest was hurting. The here and now asserted itself once again and he remembered the letters. You fell asleep! jeered a scoffing voice inside his head. You worked too late, you were careless in forgetting the flat keys. All this is your own damn fault. Christie played no part other than in keeping you alive. And this is how you treat the poor kid when like the good nurse she is she demonstrates care and concern for your well-being. Let her go home! Give her the stuff — that one to Diana especially. And make use of this night to reconcile the two images of Christie Wisdom in one and the same person. The woman you saw and in an idiotic moment thought you'd fallen for, hook, line and sinker. And the professional nurse you've come to depend upon . . .

Much more of this treatment and wild horses won't drag her back to the Manor next week!

★   ★   ★

After a rare night of tossing and turning, Christie awoke late. She'd forgotten to set her alarm! — so much for the well-organised Miss Wisdom! Yawning, she rubbed the sleep from her eyes. Every hour, on the hour, she had counted the measured chimes reverberating from the tower of St Peter's Church across the road. Had she slept at all? It didn't feel much like it, stumbling round the bedroom, bumping into chairs and dropping things in her fumbling haste.

Bundling her mass of hair into a pink gingham waterproof cap, she swished aside the shower curtain in her ivory-tiled bathroom, stepping under the spray while the water was still running chill. She almost leapt out again with a shriek, but forced herself in typical Christie fashion to grit her teeth and bear it. What a restless, frustrating night. And all thanks to Tom Galvan.

A morning shower always exhilarated Christie, set her ready to tackle the new nursing day. Water stung her cheeks as with eyes screwed tight she lifted her head to the reviving spray. Tom had seemed so withdrawn . . . aloof even. Not at all grateful that she'd remembered his letters and taken the trouble to come back and fetch them. Why, he'd made her feel a stranger to Room 27 — which was utterly ridiculous when together nurse and patient were involved in a situation of such intimacy that she could have described the small mole below his left shoulderblade and the exact location of the recent suture line; with closed eyes recall the texture of smooth olive skin and the mingled smell of sandalwood soap and warm masculinity, the way the hair curled thickly on the nape of his neck, the shape of his mouth . . .

Why, I couldn't even describe my James in such detail! Christie reflected indignantly, rubbing goose-pimpled flesh with a big blue towel.

Her hand reached automatically for the Johnson's baby talc, hesitated for an instant . . . and swapped it guiltily for the drum of Chanel No 5 talcum powder James had given her for Christmas. She dabbed herself all over with the swansdown puff, her expression far away. Today it seemed more important to smell nice than to find time for breakfast.

Years, reflected Christie dreamily, since I've seriously considered the impression I'm making on a man. Shivering a little, she slipped into delicate pink silk bra and pants, Paris designed — the one luxury Christie had retained from the old days, the softness of pure silk next to her skin. From habit she fastened the matching suspender belt at the front, swivelling the dainty gilt clasp to the hollow of her back and with rapid movements sliding pale stockings over her long slim legs. Tights were not very popular among the nurses, for the wards were hot and busy and the minimum of underwear was more comfortable beneath their uniform dresses.

Mr Galvan had looked at her so

strangely last night . . . as if he did not much care for the sight of Nurse Wisdom out of uniform, hair flopping down her back and all drab in black.

'Perhaps he'd appreciate me more in pink!'

With an ironic half-smile Christie assessed the steamy image in the bathroom mirror, trying to picture herself through another's eyes. It was difficult to be objective. At eighteen she'd been slim as bamboo, and that looked great, of course, when one was modelling a sexy Bruce Oldfield or Body Map number. Now she was certainly less bony and more womanly shaped.

At eighteen Christie's main concern had been with her appearance. As a fledgling fashion model the way she looked was bound to be all-important. She'd have laughed that she'd not a care in the world — or a serious thought in her pretty head! Spoiled and petted, the daughter of Archie Wisdom, the wealthy and celebrated theatrical impresario. At the Mayfair agency they'd praised her natural elegance but taught her how to show off couture clothes with the jazzed-up sensuality of the eighties model. Only one thing she'd ever refused, and that was to cut her hair. It was the one point on which her father had been absolutely insistent.

'Christie, whatever you choose to do in this life you know I'm right behind you. But leave your hair alone. Promise. You've no need ever to earn a living, sweetheart, but if you choose to cash in on the fact that you're a beautiful girl — just like your mother! — then go ahead and sign up for this mannequin stuff.' She'd always been able to twist him, the only daughter of his three marriages, round her little finger. 'I'll ring Wycombe Abbey and tell them you're not going back into the sixth form next term.'

Christie had total recall of that conversation. It was the first and last time she'd ever reproached her father. 'If my mother was so beautiful then why didn't you *stay* married to each other?'

He had stroked her glossy head with a rueful hand. 'I guess we drifted apart, sweetheart. One day you'll understand.'

Obstinately Christie had clung to wistful memories of those days when they were all three of them together. If *she* ever got married it was going to be once and for good, however rich and famous they both might be.

But wealth and privilege made a soft cushion for a young girl's life. Part of the year she spent in Zurich with her mother, who had remarried, this time to a Swiss banker she had known since childhood. And Archie Wisdom had brought home his third wife, Olwen, not much older than Christie herself, an aspiring opera singer he'd spied in the Glyndebourne chorus and swept off her feet and into his Knightsbridge home.

When Christie was twenty and being featured regularly in *Vogue* and *Harper's*, Archie Wisdom dropped dying to the floor of his box at Covent Garden, halfway through the second act of *Cosi Fan Tutte*; with Christie and Olwen crouching panic-stricken beside him, wringing their ineffectual hands and knowing not the least thing about first-aid. A young doctor had rushed in to help — but by then it was too late.

The event was widely reported and Christie had never been to the opera since. Music she excluded from her life. And modelling. And all things trivial.

The bulk of the estate passed to the new young widow. Christie's own inheritance was modest but sufficient to enable her to quit London and head for Hardy country to settle with a little house and a car five miles from St Joseph's. It hadn't been easy to persuade Directors of Nursing that she was serious about such a radical change of lifestyle.

Mrs Harris had been more perceptive than most. So Christabel Wisdom, fashion model, became simply Christie Wisdom, student nurse, subdued and single-minded shadow of her former carefree, vivacious self. In one night Christie felt she'd aged a lifetime. And within a few weeks of beginning training, celebrating her twenty-first birthday entirely alone, she discovered within herself the emergence of a fragile self-respect.

Archie Wisdom might be beyond saving: but his daughter was learning the hard way how to care for others.

At the start Christie's contemporaries considered her distant and solemn. Her smiles were warm but rare, and she expressed no interest in partying or the camaraderie of hospital social life, disappearing like a mysterious shadow at the end of a working day. She was different. Well, several of the student nurses owned cars — but Wisdom's was brand new and she had a cottage somewhere on the outskirts of town. And the way she walked and the poised angle of her head . . . yes, she was not Nurse Average. Something about her turned heads in spite of the fact that she obviously preferred not to draw attention to herself. Several tried, but no one could get close to Christie Wisdom.

Another peculiar thing. She was unselfish to a degree that almost seemed punishing: first to volunteer for the least popular jobs and endlessly prepared to put herself out for others. Almost desperately committed to a career that a number of the girls saw simply as a sort of VSO job — an admirable way of passing three years helping society before getting married, preferably to one of the doctors.

Christie feared in her heart that she was only masquerading as a nurse. The first few weeks seemed a never-ending torture. She even thought she'd have to quit. It seemed impossibly hard to be rushed off your feet all day and *then* expected to study and write essays at night — when all a student craved for was to flop exhausted on her bed. But gradually she toughened up, adjusted to the pace and began to relax more.

Completing the first six months of medical and surgical nursing was a milestone, followed by the tough stint on acute geriatrics — *real* nursing, in Christie's weary estimation. Practical and intermediate exams came up and were successfully passed and she earned a second stripe on her nurse's cap.

Halfway through the course, she realised with deep satisfaction that she was over the worst and nursing was in her blood for keeps. And she was becoming friendly with a doctor who seemed to be everything she'd come to respect in a man: dedicated and hardworking, far more interested in pathology than in the sort of pursuits that entertained medics like Mike Filing in their off-duty hours. He'd never set the world on fire, in the opinion of the other nurses; but in Christie's estimation you'd go a long way to discover a more dependable and dutiful partner.

★　★　★

Apart from the seductively perfumed talc which only she knew about Christie's appearance was much as usual when she set out — late — down the stepping-stone path to her garage. Well, it would look a bit obvious to start turning up with lipstick and eyeshadow and a change of hairstyle. Tom Galvan would suspect Nurse was joining his fan club.

'I'm late,' observed Christie pleasantly to the gnarled old apple tree as she knelt in the brilliantly green wet grass, gathering a fistful of forget-me-nots. 'I've never been late before. I must have caught spring fever!'

*   *   *

'It's a chest infection all right,' agreed Sir Frank Davy. 'Let's get decent levels of penicillin established quickly.' He scribbled instructions and handed the drugs record card to Christie, who raised an eyebrow and went off to get the keys to the drug trolley. The faded hothouse roses, he noted with a flicker of interest, had been replaced by a posy of forget-me-nots blue as a summer sky.

While Christie was out of the room Frank told his patient bluntly there was no chance now of returning home within the week. Tom scowled, but in truth he felt pretty awful, and though he made a token effort another bout of coughing put paid to his weary protests.

* * *

'Over on your left side, please.' Christie selected a green needle and with a dart-like flick of the wrist plunged the antibiotic into the upper outer quadrant of Tom's exposed buttock.

A show of brisk exasperation concealed the pangs of her anxiety. 'Every afternoon this room turns into Clapham Junction! Half the medical staff come tramping in to see you, loaded with germs and never a thought for the patient they're infecting with

GOK. Well, they'll have to get past *me* today.'

'Right you are, Dragon!' agreed Tom amiably, rolling over and hitching up his pyjamas with his right hand. 'But I must see my theatre team in here before the week's out. I don't feel any too lively, though: had a rotten night. They changed the bed three times, I was in such a muck sweat.'

Christie smoothed the sheets and rearranged his pillows into a comfort-able triangle. 'Stay in bed today. I'll nip down to the library and choose you something nice to take your mind off work. How about a thriller? I've just finished *Innocent Blood* and it's a fascinating read. You must have come across P. D. James.'

'Who's he?' Tom was being deliber-ately cussed. 'I only read dead authors. They're more reliable.' He exhaled a deep sigh of impatience: what a bit of rotten luck when escape had seemed just around the corner. Might as well have another stab at Engelun's paper.

'Would the library have a German dictionary, by any chance?'

Christie frowned. 'I hardly think so, Mr Galvan. What ever for?' He'd told her to call him Tom, but she felt it much wiser to keep their relationship on a strictly professional level. That way he could not so easily take advantage of his VIP position.

Tom produced from his briefcase the sheaf of photocopy paper and explained what he was trying to do, looking over Christie's shoulder as she plumped herself down on the bedspread and scanned the first page.

'"Is the mysterious pineal gland," she translated rapidly, "the brain's third eye?' Mmm, this looks rather interesting. Some of the medical terminology might prove a bit tricky, but I can certainly translate most of that for you.' Christie's beaming smile made Tom suddenly forget how lousy he'd been telling himself he was feeling. His hand rested for a moment on her smooth bare forearm as he compared her words with the German text.

'I'll make a written copy while you're resting.' She stood up hurriedly lest Tom should hear the pounding of her heartbeat, wondering for the nth time why physical closeness to this man was becoming increasingly alarming. It got worse with every passing day. Like some incurable illness.

'Nurse Wisdom, you never cease to amaze me!' he was saying admirably. 'You mean to tell me you've got A-Level German?' He didn't wait for an answer — which was just as well, since Christie had no intention of coming out with her life story. And she hadn't an A-Level to her name.

He dashed a hand through his damply curling hair. 'Well, this is a stroke of luck indeed. We'll wait till Cecilia arrives, then you can read out your translation and she can take it down in shorthand and run me off a copy on the micro.' Something ominous in Nurse Wisdom's expression warned him and he lifted an accusing finger. 'I hope you haven't — ' a fit of harsh coughing swallowed up his warning.

'Doctor's orders, Mr Galvan. No secretaries today. You are on complete bed rest . . . '

* * *

In the canteen Christie bumped into Mike Filing. 'Having a rough ride, darlin'?' he asked sympathetically, sliding a stealthy arm about Nurse Wisdom's alluring middle. 'We miss you in the Unit. When are you coming back?'

For a rash moment Christie imagined the thrill if that was someone else's hand . . . but chased the shameful thought away almost as soon as it sneaked into mind. Mike, however, sensed the second's pause before his hand was firmly removed. Encouraged, he joined her as she carried her tray of stuffed aubergine and sugarfree stewed fruit compôte to a vacant table. 'And I thought that figure was as nature intended!'

'Whatever do you mean, *Doctor*?'

Mike considered his plate of pork chop, baked beans and chips and waved his fork at Christie's choice of menu. 'I'm amazed you should need to diet. I thought that figure was nature's own.'

Christie didn't bat an eyelash; coquettish indignation was not her style. This was Mike's practised way of winding her up and she did not intend to fall for it.

He tried again, pretending to search her calm face for black eyes and bruises, insisting she was suffering from trembling hands. 'No need to be brave with me, love. Tell Uncle Mickey all about your nasty hulking patient.'

'None of your business,' came the brisk riposte. Christie finished her aubergine stuffed with rice and peppers in a savoury tomato sauce and started on her pudding. 'Could you please fill my glass with water?'

'With the greatest of pleasure,' said Mike smoothly, and emptied the full jug down Christie's front. 'Oops, sorry!' he murmured, dabbing at her soaking chest with a paper towel.

Christie stood up and swung her cloak across her shoulders, wrapping it shieldingly about her body. 'Grow up, Dr Filing,' she advised quietly, though inside she was absolutely seething, for this was the last of her clean uniforms and there was nothing for it but to wait till it dried in situ.

Up the stairs she hurried, intending to slip into the nurses' rest room on Nazareth's Corridor A, drape her sodden uniform over the radiator and tuck herself away in a quiet corner, her cloak concealing her damp underwear and her heart beating furiously over Mike Filing's spiteful display of sour grapes. She glanced quickly at her fob watch: a good ten minutes to go till she must report back on duty . . .

'Staff!' called a voice from Sister Carter's office. 'I've had a call from one of the patients on your corridor complaining of a commotion in Room

27. Would you find out what the problem is, please?'

'Oh dear!' sighed Christie, trying to pluck the clammy fabric away from her shivering skin. Whatever could have happened this time?

The heated meals trolley stood abandoned in the corridor outside Mr Galvan's open door. Inside 27, a hefty nurse with blonde-streaked hair could be seen and heard, angrily arguing the toss with Christie's cantankerous patient.

'According to my list, Mr Galvan, you most definitely ordered vanilla ice-cream for your pudding. There's nothing down here about sherry trifle. No, I can't change it now. If all of you changed your minds every five minutes — '

She had sensed Christie hovering in the doorway and half turned to exchange a grimace. Having an onlooker encouraged her to take a deep breath and attempt to regain a tone of calm persuasion. 'It's good dairy ice-cream and has a delicious flavour. Now you just try it, Mr Galvan.'

'Bah!' snorted Tom. 'Take it away, and clear off, the pair of you. Get back to your cauldron!'

'Oh, for heaven's sake!' scolded Christie, who was not her even-tempered self but struggling to push her own upset to the back of her mind.

'I'll leave you to it,' muttered the other nurse out of the corner of her mouth. 'You're not the only patient on this corridor, Mr Galvan!' she added in a sotto-voce last word.

Tom indicated the now melting dish of ice-cream and his face registered disgust. 'I did *not* order this. I'm still hungry. And I want trifle.'

Christie stood hunched in her cape, damp and uncomfortable and in no mood for sweet talk. '*I* ordered ice-cream for you,' she said flatly. 'You've had a bit of a fever. Eat it. It will soothe your throat and chest.'

Tom glowered. From beneath his eye-brows he studied Nurse Wisdom's glum expression. Sometimes she struggled not to smile when he put on one of his rude impossible moods. Not this time. She looked sad and somehow vulnerable. He tried again to make her smile, poking at the pudding dish with a fastidious forefinger. 'Take this away. It's disgusting. Tastes like bone marrow!'

Sticking out a foot, Christie kicked the door shut behind her. 'I am sick to death,' she announced crossly, 'of tiresome doctors.' She stalked forward to take the plate away and as her hand reached out her cloak slipped off her shoulders.

Tom stared in fascination, blinked, and stared again. 'Hell's teeth, Gertie, you're practically showing your breakfast!' His eyes gleamed beneath narrowed lids. This certainly made up for the pudding disappointment! 'Enjoy your swim?'

The white uniform had turned transparent. Hands on hips, Christie glanced down and was infuriated to see pink bra, bikini briefs and suspenders on full display. 'That is Dr Filing for you,' she said tight-lipped. 'He tipped a jug of water over me.'

Tom's guffaw ricocheted off all four walls. 'Trying to cool you off, was he, Gertie?'

Hugging her arms protectively across herself, Christie felt her teeth begin to chatter. 'I already have a b-b-boy friend, as you know perfectly well. What Mike Filing can't seem to g-grasp is that I find him quite resistible!'

A wave of anger consumed Tom, an internal fury that had nothing to do with his already raised temperature. He was on his feet, reaching out to put his good arm about her shivering form and draw her close, the instinct of a strong man to protect the weaker sex.

As his dark shadow loomed over her, coming between her and daylight, Christie for one fleeting second felt threatened. Then she felt the comfortingly protective weight of his arm and saw the kindness and concern in his eyes, the old Tom, the Tom people spoke of with such warm, affectionate admiration. Burning tears seared her eyelids and her soft mouth trembled as she remembered the hostility in Mike Filing's eye. It was all she could do to stop herself burying her head against Tom's shoulder and breaking down completely.

'You must get out of these wet clothes,' encouraged Tom, his chin grazing the top of her trembling cap. 'Just as well I didn't turn off the bathroom radiator. Your things will dry in no time.' As he spoke his hand was unfastening the press studs down the front of her dress and Christie was somehow too dazed to stop him, though the impropriety of the whole situation, a patient undressing a nurse, was too horrific to contemplate. But this *wasn't* a patient, but a doctor; and the authority of his voice and practised hands held her totally in thrall.

Her dress slid off her shoulders and Tom with a click of his tongue observed that her silken underwear was soaked right through. It was pretty startling sort of underwear for a nurse to be able to afford, let alone wear for work . . .

It couldn't be for his benefit, could it? A put-up job to lure the neuro-surgeon into a one-armed affair?

Meditatively Tom eyed the tempting person of Nurse Wisdom en déshabillé. Couldn't do myself justice at the moment, Gertie darling. More sensible to wait till the plaster cast comes off. Though I'm bound to confess you're in spectacular shape.

And she seemed such a cool-eyed young lady! Yet clearly she must have driven one of the SHOs to make a spiteful display of his frustration.

A corner of his mouth twisted in amusement. There was one sure way to find out.

Experimentally he placed a deliberate hand over her right breast. Christie gasped in outrage and was out of his grasp on the instant.

It was answer enough.

He grinned openly as an accusatory

'Mr Galvan!' exploded from her dry lips. He saw her arm lift and draw back to slap his face, but he was too tall and too fast-reacting for her to manage it successfully. Steely fingers manacled Christie's narrow wrist even as her hand moved in mid-air. And at that very moment the two of them froze as the door handle rattled and Sister Carter's voice, tinged with excitement, said, 'Here we are, Dr Diamond — Room 27. What a wonderful surprise for our dear Mr Galvan!'

6

'Into the bathroom!'

Christie grabbed her uniform and fled.

As one door opened the other closed, and only Tom heard the click of the lock. As if her life depended on it, Christie turned the key and sank down upon the rim of the bath, her fingers gripping its cold edge.

Annoyance and curiosity warred in her mind. She had yet to report for duty! What on earth would Sister Carter make of her apparent absence? And here she was, trapped in a patient's bathroom with — from the sound of it — little prospect of escape. A heartily polite conversation was taking place on the other side of the door; Diana Diamond's famous, precise tones telling of her trans-Atlantic dash to spend just one day at Tom's bedside, so as to convince herself he was well and truly on the mend.

Christie tossed her head at this: And a pity you didn't make the effort sooner, Dr Diamond!

She stripped off her wet clothes, spreading them along the radiator, wrapping herself in a warm dry bathtowel she had laundered herself.

If Tom were *my* fiancé, wild horses wouldn't have kept me away! let alone some wretched television film.

An awful thought struck Christie and her hand stifled a rising groan. If Diana planned to spend the rest of the day in Room 27, how on *earth* was she to get out? At some point the woman would wish to use the bathroom — and then what? Exposure!

Sister was speaking commiseratingly of jet-lag and a visit she'd made three years ago to her married sister in Vancouver. Dr Diamond's response sounded ever so slightly impatient: as if she couldn't wait to be left alone with Tom.

Her voice floated nearer and a rich strange smell seeped round the edges of the bathroom door. Wrinkling her nose as she tried to identify what it could be, Christie realised Dr Diamond must have walked around the bed and was now standing close beside Tom's uninjured arm. She'd picked up the case notes and was quizzing Sister Carter about his chest infection. Tom hawked pitifully and Christie almost giggled out loud as Sister told him to cut that out unless he wanted a clip round the ear.

Sister agreed that yes, this was a slight setback which had given rise to some anxiety; but that as Dr Diamond must surely appreciate, Mr Galvan was receiving the finest specialist care. Adding with a smile in her voice that the neuro-surgeon was being treated like a piece of rare Meissen porcelain, to be mended good as new. With an absolutely first-rate nurse assigned to monitor his progress each hour of the day.

In the bathroom the first-rate nurse pulled a comical face. Meissen porcelain indeed!

'Where is this paragon, then?' Dr Diamond sounded tartly unimpressed. 'Do your nurses usually leave their clothes in patients' rooms?'

At this Christie almost jumped out of her skin. But Tom smoothly intervened. 'Christie's doing something rather urgent just this moment — I hope that's okay with you, Carol. I believe you asked her to come up during her lunch break, and I'm afraid I took advantage of her kind nature. She must have forgotten her cloak.'

Phew, that was a close one! The unwilling eavesdropper had to smile. It was masterfully done, the implication being that Christie was occupied with vital business on the neuro-surgeon's behalf. Now no one would be wondering where she had got to. For a while at any rate.

Christie exhaled with relief. She'd have liked to get a peep at Diana Diamond through the keyhole, but it meant removing the key and that would be too dangerous. She'd have to rely on her imagination.

On TV Diana always wore the same outfit, but in a variety of brilliant Liberty silks in abstract patterns. Never florals, for she was not that sort of a woman. This unvarying style had clearly been designed to be time-saving for the presenter yet glamorously eye catching: a thigh-length silk tunic, tight-sleeved and with a shallow neckline, worn over loose pants tapering to a narrow ankle that emphasised the daintiness of Diana's size three feet and her exquisite taste in shoes. At the close of each programme she would perch on a high stool, like the best of teachers summing up for her audience the essence of what had gone before, one slender heel hooked over the rung of her stool, occasionally gesticulating in character-istic fashion with two hands forming a steeple, her hair a bonfire of gelled Rossetti curls and her face the face of a Star.

Vivacious and confident she looked and sounded. No wonder she'd been picked for the job. No wonder she'd captivated the heart of a fascinating rogue like Tom Galvan.

You could scrape her make-up off with a trowel, remembered Christie. Don't I know all about *that*! I wonder if she ever lets Tom see her without her warpaint? Now I look nothing without blusher and a palette of eyeshadows. But if I wanted to I could turn myself back into a face out of *Vogue*: it's easy when you've got totally forgettable features.

It's funny to think about it, but in a way, Diana Diamond and I are poles apart. I've given up the glamour for nursing. And she's given up practising medicine for the glamour. Awful woman. How could she abandon her profession? All that money wasted on training her to be a doctor.

With an effort Christie pulled herself out of her reverie. It made for uncomfortable listening: but if she didn't, how would she know if a chance cropped up to creep out unobserved?

Something was different. The voices were quieter, more intimate . . . murmurings and rustling silences. Sister had gone at last, leaving Tom and Diana alone together. And it didn't require much imagination to picture what was going on now! Diana and Tom in each other's arms, making up for lost time.

Christie turned pink with embarrassment. Tom knew his nurse was but a few feet away; that a mere ten minutes before it had been Christie herself sheltering within the circle of his good arm. He'd be chuckling inside at her predicament. If ever a man had a warped sense of humour it was he.

'I'm not going to listen. I'm not, I'm not.' Christie talked busily to herself, rapidly putting on her now dry clothing, listing in her head all the tasks she must get through as soon she escaped from the hot little bathroom. Tom and Diana. Diana and Tom. Diana of the red roses. Christie and James.

'You'll stay at the flat tonight, of course.' That was Tom, speaking in a more normal pitch.

'I thought I would — I've got my keys. Anything you want me to bring over for you? How about a cassette player and some of your opera tapes?'

'Better not.' Tom sounded gloomy, as if the idea appealed but must be resisted.

'Well, what about some books? By the way, how are you getting your washing done? Pyjamas and towels and things?'

Now he was surprised. 'My washing? Funny, Diana, but I hadn't given that a thought.' There was a significant pause. 'Seems to be doing itself.' A tentative-sounding knock interrupted the discussion. 'Yes? Come in!'

'Oh, I am sorry!' apologised a delighted-looking nurse, goggling at Dr Diamond. 'I was wondering, Mr Galvan, if you knew where Staff Wisdom could be found? I didn't realise you had — er — a visitor.'

'As you can see, she's not here.' There was a teasing gleam in Galvan's eye. 'Anything else we can help you with, Nurse? Don't be afraid to ask.'

'It's a frightful cheek, I know, Mr Galvan, but I was wondering if Dr Diamond would give me her autograph.'

'Dr Diamond's autograph? You mean to tell me you don't want mine?'

The nurse giggled and blushingly admitted, 'Well, Mr Galvan, you are pretty famous around these parts, but — er — '

Diana put a stop to Tom's teasing. 'I'd be delighted. Now what am I to write on? Your cap! What a droll idea, duckie. Hope you've got another. I generally put, 'Wishing you the Best of Health' — what's your Christian name? . . . Sarah. There you are.'

'Oh, thanks tons, Dr Diamond!'

Christie heard the door close, and then Tom's voice, clearly amused, commented, 'Quite the celebrity, aren't you, Diana darling? Does it still give you a thrill, my little pocket Venus, or are you really as blasé as you appear?'

Diana hated being reminded that she stood but five feet one in her tiny stockinged feet. She might be small, but her personality was anything but. She changed the subject. 'These roses ought to be in water. Don't you think they're a glorious colour? I bought them because they reminded me of that wonderful Portuguese sun . . . mm . . . remember, darling?

'Is that your bathroom through there? Perhaps there's a vase — '

The voice that unflinchingly revealed to the nation the most intimate workings of the human body sounded but inches from Christie's horrified ear. The door handle moved under the pressure of Diana's fingers. 'Funny, it seems to be locked.'

'Diana, do leave those for my nurse. She sees to all that. Give the girl something to do, for heaven's sake. There's little enough to keep her busy as it is. Ridiculous, the idea that I require full-time nursing!'

'I hope she's fair, fat and forty. I know what you are, Tom Galvan.'

Christie exhaled in relief as she heard Diana move away from the door. There was a creak of bedsprings as Diana sat down. She was checking Tom's recent surgery, examining the plastered arm, asking questions, taking his pulse — very much the professional doctor.

When did he think he would be back in business? He must have been terribly depressed? Was there any loss of feeling in the hand or fingers?

Then apparently having satisfied herself that no lasting damage had been sustained, Diana reverted to a sexually teasing intimacy. 'Have you missed me?' Her voice was muffled and beguiling, and Christie stared hard at the frosted glass of the window and tried not to listen as Tom joined in with most inconsiderate gusto, teasing his companion about her exploits in the USA.

'We're both adults, aren't we?'

murmured Diana provocatively. 'What the eye doesn't see the heart doesn't grieve over . . . we've never pretended to be saints. Ouch, Tom Galvan, you know how easily I bruise! Look, when is this nurse of yours coming back? I want to have a word with her about you. In private. Stop it . . . and mind those roses!'

Tom had a brainwave. 'Why don't you take a look in the sluice? Isn't that where vases are kept?'

As soon as she heard 27's door open Christie was out in a flash. Avoiding Tom's eye, she grabbed up her cloak and fled down to the office to report herself back on duty.

'Mr Galvan has a visitor,' beamed Sister Carter, 'his fiancée, Dr Diana Diamond. I've told her what a splendid job you've been doing. Perhaps you've already seen her?'

'No, Sister,' said Christie truthfully.

'Then I'm sure you would like to introduce yourself.'

Better get it over with, thought

Christie resignedly. Her legs felt like lead and her head throbbed. She took the lift up to Corridor B, wishing this awful day would get itself over with quickly.

Brightening at the thought, she realised she was now free to help out with other patients since for the rest of the afternoon Tom had his own private doctor dancing attendance. It had hit home, his remark that there was little in his care and treatment to occupy a full-time nurse. Soon he would be discharged, and she could escape from Nazareth Wing and get back to being a stopgap nurse on the achingly busy hospital wards. Perhaps this time with a permanent contract under her staff nurse's belt!

Conscious that her heart was thumping quite ridiculously at the prospect of coming face to face with the woman who held Tom Galvan's heart, Christie slipped into the cloakroom for a moment to regain her poise with a few deep-breathing exercises.

The face in the mirror didn't seem to match the nervousness within. It looked back at her gravely, ivory-pale, with tranquil mouth and melting dark eyes. She wished she had some rosy blusher in her bag. Beside Diana she would be a washed-out shadow. At least her hair was neat, her cap set straight — and her clothes dry. 'Come in!' Tom's deep voice commanded at her polite knock.

He lay enthroned among his pillows like a monarch graciously receiving homage. A vase of golden roses had been placed on the table across the foot of his bed. And by the window lounged a small but vivid figure, sporting prominent cerise earrings and a shiny cerise shirt with built-in shoulder pads, worn loose and baggy over clinging black ski pants. The celebrated television doctor.

'Back at last, Gertie. We thought you'd got lost.' Tom winked and raised an amused eyebrow as he saw his nurse's shoulders give a huffy little wiggle in response. 'Diana — this is Staff Nurse Wisdom. Gertie, I call her. But Christine is her real name.'

'Christabel, actually. How do you do, Dr Diamond.'

Diana had been eyeing her with a peculiar intensity from the moment she walked through the door. Christie was very aware of that. But now the other woman unfolded her arms and came forward to greet her, her right hand outstretched and her grip firm and warm as they shook hands.

It was a strange moment. And with it Christie's distrust of Diana Diamond entirely disappeared. The voice was the same. But Diana in the flesh was . . . different. And she was wearing some remarkably unusual perfume, heady and disturbing in close proximity.

'I hear you've been marvellous. No doctor was ever an easy patient.'

Tom watched closely as the two women conversed. They made such a contrasting pair. Even her ill-fitting uniform couldn't disguise the nurse's pale slender elegance and natural manner. She didn't appear to be overawed at walking into his room and finding herself face to face with *the* Diana Diamond. She didn't gush or stammer, or in any way seem anything but the same old Gertie.

Pretty cool of her, applauded Tom, considering she must have spent the past twenty minutes locked in his bathroom chewing her fingernails to the quick!

He removed her cap, pulled out the hairpins, made her shake her head till the silky hair swung loose and free down her back . . . Swopped the white dress for a short scarlet satin sheath and sheer black stockings. Why bother with shoes? The legs looked terrific . . . consign those sensible lace-ups to the nurses' locker room. A touch of lipstick on the widely curved mouth? Okay, but leave it at that. For every time she came close to him Tom had been conscious of a longing to touch that perfect skin and see if it was for real.

Funny thing about Gertie. In uniform she was Nurse with a capital N. In scarlet satin she made Tom forget he was in love with Diana.

Diana was adept at setting others at their ease. She chatted easily to Nurse Wisdom, who was clearly as competent and thorough as Frank and the others had insisted. Nothing to look at, but a very nice, kind girl, with an interesting streak of firmness that was in Tom's best interests.

The accident had changed him. That was inevitable when a man came close to death yet survived. He'd be more compassionate. Perhaps less confident for a while till he got back into the swing of things. And more determined about the way he saw his life heading. Diana knew she hadn't been mistaken about what she had seen in Tom's eyes this afternoon. After all these years he was going to demand she made her mind up, yes or no. And what was she going to say, when even in her heart of hearts she didn't know?

Contributing little to the conversation — Diana was asking questions about the night of the accident — from his vantage point at the apex of a triangle Tom could watch, contrast and compare. Two women who were closely involved with him: the one emotionally, the other professionally. He concentrated on Diana.

She hadn't always been this highly sophisticated woman whose media successes had bestowed upon her boundless confidence. Come a long, long way, hadn't she, from the teenager he had first fallen for, puppy-fat and all, with her hooting, infectious laugh and effervescent personality.

When Di at first declared she was going in for surgery there'd been the usual jokes about standing her on an orange box so she could see over the edge of the operating table. But she attacked work like a Trojan and she'd been just as driven by ambition; if a woman could make it in surgery it would be Diana Diamond. What no one foresaw was that inside the extrovert little medical student lurked this Titian-tressed TV goddess in cerise silk-satin and pink suede Manolo Blahnik shoes. The most famous woman doctor in the British Isles.

She's terrific! marvelled Christie. Not awful at all. She's perfect for Tom Galvan. Razor-sharp and formidable. An amazing woman. About as different from the likes of me as you could hope to find.

As usual, I had it all wrong. Meeting Diana has been an eye-opener for me . . . perhaps you *don't* have to scrub your face to show you're serious about life, don't have to cut out all the frills. Could it be I've been *too* determined, too puritanical? Too rejecting of the past?

With a lump in her throat Christie left Tom's room to make herself useful on Corridor B. It would be a relief to occupy her mind with patients other than Mr Galvan. She'd be glad when this job was complete — it was dangerously claustrophobic to be so wrapped up in the welfare of one extremely attractive man. You'd have to be a professed nun, she mused wryly, not to get led into foolish fantasies. Fantasies finally revealed for what they were, with the reality of Diana Diamond.

★ ★ ★

A light was on in the linen cupboard and a trolley stood just inside the doorway. Christie poked her head in to find Sarah Thorne struggling to reach down pillowcases from the top rack. 'Hi, Sarah, let me do that for you — at school they didn't call me Willowy Wisdom for nothing. How many of these do you want? Here you are, half a dozen. My patient,' she added wryly, 'has a VIP visitor, so I've come to make myself useful.'

Sarah looked relieved. 'I've had two patients in for day surgery. They're going home any minute, so we can get the rooms ready for tomorrow's admissions.' She dumped a pile of sheets on the trolley and confided with a delighted grin, 'To tell the truth, I'm a bit behind because I've been talking to Diana Diamond, your VIP! She signed her autograph on my cap. Look, I've got it here.'

From the bottom shelf of the trolley she produced a creased rectangle that had once been folded into a disposable white hat but which now bore the flourishing well wishes of Diana Diamond. 'Christie, that woman is absolutely stunning! I've never stood so close to such a glamorous human being in all my life. Mind you, you can see she's all of thirty. Roll on thirty, sez I!'

Sarah switched off the light and shut the door, and the two nurses set off down the corridor, Christie wheeling the linen skip and following the linen trolley to the first vacated room. 'You ought to volunteer to show her round Nazareth. Go on. She might like to do a documentary on private medicine and we'd all appear on telly. Remember when Frank Bough and the BBC did those programmes from the Portsmouth hospitals?'

Sarah was such a chatterbox it was like a breath of fresh air after the earlier trauma of this afternoon. Together they changed the beds and swabbed down the lockers — it still had to be done even though they had scarcely been touched.

* * *

'Mr Hadfield next — haemorrhoidectomy. Oral lubricant prescribed and daily saline baths. We'll just check he's comfortable.' They knocked and a man's cheerful voice bade them enter.

'Hello, ladies,' said the patient, peering at the nurses over a pink *Financial Times*. 'Do you know, this op's not half as bad as they made out at the golf club. My surgeon says I shall be completely over it within a fortnight.'

Sarah had whipped the metal cap off a bottle of Guinness and was expertly pouring the drink into a tall glass. 'That's right, Mr Hadfield. And in the meantime we want you to drink plenty of these to build you up!'

'Build me up?' exclaimed the big man. 'Strewth! My wife will have something to say about that.'

Christie explained as they tidied the bed that apart from being good for him the Guinness would have a mild laxative effect which would help the sore surgical area. 'Now, are you quite comfortable? Anything else you need? Afternoon tea will be arriving shortly.'

The elderly lady with the cataract, scheduled for surgery first thing the next morning, was peacefully sleeping, so the nurses didn't disturb her.

Someone rang their bell and Sarah hurried off to answer it, leaving Christie to change the dressing on Andrew Tate, a university student, still drowsy from the anaesthetic of his sinus operation late that morning. He was coughing gobs of blood and mucus into a disposable vomit bowl, and Christie wiped his mouth with a tissue and settled a clean pad under his nostrils, looping the strings over his ears and fastening them beneath his chin. No Hot Drinks, warned the sign above his bed.

'Any pain in your stomach?'

Andrew retched again. He shook his head. 'You don't have to put up with this, you know,' said Christie sympathetically. 'I can give you an injection.'

'It's okay,' he spluttered. 'My nose doesn't hurt — just the back of my head.'

'I'm afraid that's the anaesthetic.' Christie checked the drugs chart. 'I see you've been given paracetamol. It will soon take effect.' At this moment the door opened and a tentative middle-aged couple hovered on the threshold. 'Mr and Mrs Tate?' welcomed Christie with a smile. 'Do please come on in. Your son has had his operation, and as you see everything's going well.'

As she hastened down the corridor she realised her forehead was throbbing, but put it down to the tension of the day. It was time to see to her own patient, VIP visitor or no.

With her fingers resting coolly on Mr Galvan's pulse and a very practised eye following the second hand of her watch, it was difficult to exclude the conversation the two were carrying on as if Christie were just part of the furniture.

'What shall you do about supper tonight? Cook yourself something at the flat?'

'I'm dining,' said Diana, 'with Frank Davy. His new lady-friend's doing the cooking, so I understand.'

'His *what*?'

Diana shrugged. 'Have I said something I shouldn't have?'

'Well, he's not mentioned anything to me.'

'*Pas devant* . . . ' mouthed Diana, suddenly conscious of Nurse Wisdom's presence. Christie didn't let this faze her but carried on with apparent disregard, though inside she felt prickly as a gooseberry.

'Can't you stay at least till the weekend?' demanded Tom.

Diana did something rather fierce with her feline amber eyes. 'Darling, you know I wish I could.'

'This woman,' Tom was appealing to Christie now. She really wished he wouldn't. 'This woman is obsessed by Work. She has a radio in her head which is always on and always tuned to the same wavelength.'

Christie screwed the cap back on her pen and tucked it into her breast pocket. A case of the pot calling the kettle black! she considered to herself ironically, refusing to be drawn into whatever quarrel might be brewing between her patient and his fiancée.

Dr Diamond was leaning back in the window chair, fingers thrust into the thick curly mass of her bright hair, swinging a pink suede toe and with a catlike smile on her glossy plum-red mouth. She had a low boredom threshold and restlessness was already gnawing at the edges of her patience. She'd been idle for too long. And though Tom was clearly in one piece and on the mend, he was not half the usual fun caged in a hospital room and with his left arm still in plaster.

His nurse had little to say for herself. Yet Diana sensed a bond of real liking between the two of them. Nothing to worry about, though. Not the sort of woman to divert Tom Galvan.

Pale, severe-looking girl; no attempt to make anything of herself.

Just as well, mused Diana, watching the nurse's every move from beneath lowered lids. She knew she'd been lucky so far. Neither of them pretended to be saints, but she was pretty certain Tom was generally far too busy himself to seek more than the odd idle flirtation. But he was beginning to turn demanding. Talking of the two of them settling down at the Manor. Diana didn't want to give in yet: not at the height of her career. No, this girl was safe enough.

No competition here.

Christie picked up her tray and was pleasantly surprised to find Diana waiting to open the door for her. She was even more surprised when the doctor suddenly materialised at her side, the rich strange smell of her perfume filling the treatment room and swamping the odour of antiseptic.

'Poison!' said Christie sharply. Of course, that was it — Poison.

And with that one small exclamation; Dr Diamond received the first inkling that where Christie Wisdom was concerned, she just *might* have made an important error of judgement.

7

'Yes,' agreed Diana, raising a feathery eyebrow in surprise, 'clever girl! It *is* Poison — the latest Dior perfume. Berries and things as well as the usual flowers. What do you think of it?'

'On you — stunning!' said Christie simply. 'Not everyone could wear it. I certainly couldn't.'

No, dear, brooded the other speculatively. Because you're not in my league. Lily-of-the-valley would be more your style. But now you do have me puzzled. You're more street-wise than I first took you for, more sophisticated. I'm a celebrity, so why aren't you stammering and blushing? My reputation generally has the effect of making people excited and nervous. But you're not overawed by the fact that I'm famous; in fact you're cool as the proverbial cucumber. It might be worth looking into your background . . . Nurse Wisdom.

Diana continued to stare, arms folded, amber eyes narrow, assessing the other woman. There's respect there, she mused, but you're not going to grovel. Fair enough. I don't thrive on it. But I do want to hang on to Tom. And now all of a sudden I'm not so sure if it's safe to let you hang about him much longer. At thirty-four Tom's wanting to settle down. Our 'arrangement' is beginning to pall. He might be fair game for a clever girl who plays her cards right.

At first glance, Wisdom, you looked a proper plain Jane. Now, close to, I see you're not. And you've got intelligence and spirit. I'm beginning to wonder: is this such a good idea after all?

Diana's watchful silence was puzzling to Christie, who carried on tidying things away and closing cupboards till everything was neat and orderly. Was the doctor worried about Tom's work, perhaps?

'You won't need me to tell you this,'

she offered out of quiet concern that Dr Diamond should appreciate the torment the neuro-surgeon had gone through, 'but in spite of the fact that he was dreadfully injured Mr Galvan has never let up in his concern with his work. His sense of frustration has been profound, and at one time he was severely depressed. I expect you also heard,' she added with a wry smile, 'how he got *that* out of his system by giving the nursing staff hell. He may not be able to operate at the moment, but I can assure you that — much to my dismay! — he continues to run the department of neuro-surgery from Room 27. The problem is to make sure he gets sufficient rest to recuperate properly.'

So don't be impatient with him for turning out to be as human and vulnerable as the next man, blazed the message in the intent brown eyes. Don't lose interest. Don't fall out of love because Tom can't be his old dynamic self till that plaster comes off. Love him in sickness, Dr Diamond, as well as in health. But don't come here for a flying visit to unsettle my patient and make him uncertain of your future together. More than ever he needs the support and reassurance of your love.

Diana was intrigued by the steadiness of the other's gaze, so clearly conveying more than the spoken word — intrigued, and more disturbed than ever. This girl was totally involved with Tom's welfare.

She shook herself mentally, chiding herself for being over-suspicious. Of *course* Wisdom must be committed and concerned. She was Joseph's trained, wasn't she, and according to the bosses first-rate at her job. The Nursing Process taught the eighties' nurse to use his or her intelligence; to consider the psychological effects of illness, and how circumstances might affect each individual patient's behaviour. Tom's case, thought Diana shrewdly, must be unusually complicated and interesting. But that didn't mean Wisdom was ready to jump into bed with the guy, for Pete's sake!

Feeling much less disquieted now, she came straight to the point. 'Would you be prepared to go home with your patient when he is discharged next week?'

Oh-oh! said Christie to herself, forewarned by what she had read in Mr Galvan's case notes. No way, she'd promised at the time. But that had been in the early days when she hardly knew whether she was coming or going because of the surgeon's infuriating behaviour.

'I understand your contract finishes at the close of this case. And that you're in line for appointment to a staff-nurse post from the first of July.'

Christie raised an eyebrow, surprised that Dr Diamond should be so much better informed about her future than she was herself. Thanks very much, she mused ironically, for letting me know!

'Of course,' suggested the other mockingly, 'you may feel you deserve to take a holiday after nursing such a difficult patient.'

'I have two weeks due,' agreed Christie slowly, 'but I hadn't made any plans.' She stood with her hands clasped in front of her apron, her lowered eye-lashes concealing her expression while Diana tapped an impatient foot.

'We can give you twenty-four hours to come to a decision. Sir Frank Davy is quite definite that Tom must not go back to the Manor unless he's accompanied by a private nurse. It's a beautiful spot, very remote and tranquil. Just the sort of place to convalesce — *so long as* Tom doesn't overdo things. Which he will, of course, you can bet on it. Fall off a horse or something and break the other arm. He enjoys taking risks. I guess that's why he became a neuro-surgeon.'

Christie sighed at the mental vision of herself hanging on to Tom's bridle and shrieking 'Over my dead body, Mr Galvan!' More hassle. 'I'll need a ball and chain,' she murmured pessimistically.

Diana clapped both hands together in triumph, her earlier qualms apparently quite forgotten. 'You'll take the job, then. Great. That's settled.'

She was all animation as she hustled Christie towards the door. 'I shall tell Tom he's to be discharged after all on Tuesday. I haven't much time and his housekeeper will need to be informed. Sir Frank will be most relieved you've agreed to go.' Anyone would think you were the only reliable nurse in the place! she added to herself cynically.

★   ★   ★

James and Christie sat down to supper. 'I've made your favourite tonight — spinach and mushroom lasagne. With steamed haricots verts, grown and frozen with my own fair hands. Cheer up, James dear! Matilda will come too, and I'm told it's only a twenty-minute drive down the motorway. I daresay I shall be permitted the occasional exeat.'

'It's not *that*,' protested James,

unfurling a damask napkin and spreading it across his knees. 'Anyway, I shouldn't presume to interfere in your career. No, I'm proud you should be asked — that everyone thinks so highly of you. Lovely, thanks. Mmm, smells good. I didn't get time for lunch today.'

Christie laid a hand on his wrist. 'Go steady with the salt, love — it's well seasoned. So tell me, why are you so down in the mouth tonight?'

James drained his glass and refilled it with frothy red Lambrusco. His sigh was weary with futility. 'Today in the post-mortem room I removed healthy kidneys that could have saved two lives. But . . . ' he gestured helplessly with outspread hands, 'the families refused permission for them to be used.'

Deep furrows scarred his brow, and Christie noticed with a pang black rings shadowing his tired bespectacled eyes. Poor James. A lump formed in her throat and her appetite shrivelled away to nothing.

'When I think of the poor souls being

cared for on the renal ward, waiting and praying for a chance to live — ' he shook his head in helpless anguish.

They both stared at their plates as if the food had turned to sawdust.

'I sometimes wonder,' he continued slowly, 'if I'm doing anything useful at all.'

'But you can't seriously mean that!' Christie clutched at his arm, conscious of how thin he was beneath the hand-knitted olive wool sweater. 'Pathology tests are very necessary for the work the clinicians are doing. Doctors like you are indispensable. Oh, James darling, never doubt yourself. You have your research — '

He put his hand over hers and managed a smile. 'And, thank heaven, I have you.' Christie rested her head on his shoulder feeling strangely weak and drained. Together they managed to finish the meal with some semblance of enjoyment.

'Promise me one thing: that you'll take up your holiday entitlement before you sign any permanent contract. You've had no break and you were on duty over Christmas and the New Year. Tell me, how long are you expecting to be tied up with Galvan?'

'Till early June when the plaster comes off.' Christie spooned fresh orange jelly on to two plates and wished she'd bought some thick cream to enrich James's portion. 'Mr Galvan will want to get back to Joe's the minute he's capable of operating. I could take a fortnight then: go and stay in Sussex with Olwen.' See Ben, she thought, and a lump rose in her throat. 'Olwen's singing at Glyndebourne this season. Not a major rôle yet, of course, but she's thrilled to have the part of Frasquita in *Carmen*.'

'If only I wasn't absolutely tone-deaf I'd offer to take you to a performance,' said James. Now *there*, he mused regretfully, would be a place to propose! What could be more romantic than a summer evening at Glyndebourne, picnicking by the lake, strolling through the gardens . . .

But as for sitting through *Carmen* — there were limits for a non-music lover! Besides, Christie had ambitions as serious as his own; she wouldn't wish to marry till she'd been made a Sister with a ward of her own. It would be unfair to ask her. She was such a kind and thoughtful girl. Might even say yes, just to avoid hurting his feelings.

James's spirits drooped further, for he was nothing if not a man of conscience. You couldn't marry someone and then turn round and say, I'm sorry, dear! But I'm going to have to leave you . . .

Christie's expression was sad and faraway. 'My father took me to Glyndebourne when I was sixteen. It was Mozart — *Il Seraglio*.' She shivered at the barrage of painful memories. In all her life she never wanted to go to the opera again. 'We were quite a large party. I had a marvellous time. But I shan't go to *Carmen*.'

Olwen will be disappointed, nudged her conscience. But you'd rather babysit, wouldn't you? Have Ben all to yourself for a few hours, give the nanny a night off.

James saw that a change of subject was called for. 'So, you'll be away to this place of Galvan's on Tuesday. What do you intend to do about the cottage? Do you think it's wise to leave this place empty for any length of time?'

'Oh dear! I haven't given a thought to the practicalities. I'm afraid I let myself be steamrollered by the redoubtable Dr Diamond. In fact, I don't even recall agreeing to take the job!' She was biting her lip, twisting her glossy mane of hair into one thick braid snaking over the shoulder of her loose-fitting grey sweatshirt.

An hour later when James drove back to his flat it was all arranged. He would move in on the Tuesday with a few belongings, to caretake while Christie was away.

It was the ideal solution, and in her mind she felt far happier about the whole proposition, pulling her duvet up to her chin and for the first time that day with the leisure to mull over what she had now taken on.

In her head Christie listed the plus points.

Escape from those striking and watchful eyes which either totally ignored her or monitored her every move. Escape from the charged and claustrophobic atmosphere of Room 27; the enforced proximity which had led to dangerous and reprehensible dreams about Tom Galvan. Dreams quite beyond her control; dreams intense and peculiar, fuelled by her subsconscious desires.

Christie sighed into the grainy darkness. Why didn't she dream like that about James? James, the man she hoped to marry.

But at least she had the sense to recognise her problem for what it was. A silly schoolgirl crush. On a terrifically fanciable man who had every red-blooded female at Joe's sighing over him like a big-screen idol.

Why, even the Chief Nursing Officer would succumb if she had to nurse Tom Galvan for weeks on end! Christie giggled into her pillow and felt much better for the vision of a lovesick Mrs Harris making sheep's eyes at the neuro-surgeon over her bifocals.

Nothing to it, gal. Just pull yourself together. Be tough with yourself — you've had plenty of practice in self-denial over the past few years.

Christie's throat felt unnaturally dry. She got up to fetch a drink of water from the bathroom and stared at her lustrous-eyed reflection in the mirror over the washbasin. How pink her cheeks looked tonight, all rosy and healthy! She padded back to bed on bare feet, setting the glass where she could easily reach it on the white cane bedside table.

Her head seemed to be floating six inches above the pale blue pillowslip. Yet her limbs were leaden with fatigue. All will come right at the Manor, she reassured herself drowsily. The nurse-patient relationship will lose its intensity in all that lovely space. Tom and I won't be shut up together any more. There'll be space between the two of us. Space to see things in perspective. And it will lessen the impact of the final break between us . . .

For in her heart, and only within the secrecy of the four silent walls of her convent-like bedroom, dared Christie acknowledge the truth that she cared far too deeply about this patient. She must be the one to nurse him back to full health and strength.

★　★　★

Wrapped in her navy cloak, Staff Nurse Wisdom awaited instructions in Sister Carter's office on the Nazareth Wing.

'Mr Galvan was discharged earlier than planned.'

'Which nurse went home with him?' asked Christie faintly.

'It wasn't necessary. Dr Diamond flew with him to the South of France and they've been staying in a rented house near the Mediterranean. If you're sure you feel up to it the job's still open. I forget which day he's due home, but we can easily find that out. The question is, Wisdom, are you fit? We've been most concerned about you.'

'It was only the 'flu, Sister Carter.'

'And a particularly nasty virus, so Dr Mallory has told me. Fortunately only you and Sarah Thorne succumbed this time.'

'Oh lord, poor Sarah!'

'These things happen. I was thankful Dr Diamond took control of the situation. With you ill I should have had quite a staffing problem on my hands. I was highly relieved, I can tell you,' confided Carol Carter with a wry chuckle, 'when Dr Diamond suggested taking Tom to convalesce in the South of France.'

But Christie was puzzled. 'How odd.' What could have made the TV doctor change her mind?

'*Odd*, nurse? Why odd?'

'Well, peculiar, I mean. I got the distinct impression Dr Diamond was far too busy to take time off from her television work.'

'She certainly didn't race here to visit him, did she? Perhaps — ' The telephone on her desk shrilled and Sister picked up the receiver. 'Yes? Yes, indeed. She's right here in my office. Nine-thirty?' Sister glanced at her watch. 'It's almost that now. Okay. Will do.'

She beamed at Christie. 'Mrs Harris would like to see you. Good news, I believe. Trot along right away. But remember I'm expecting you with me for the rest of the day, so don't let her go sending you back to Casualty!'

★   ★   ★

Christie pulled into the verge of the now gently climbing road and with the engine still running studied her one-inch map. She must be somewhere near the left-hand turn. Half a mile, perhaps? Checking in the rear-view mirror, she moved off, blinking against the golden sunlight of a perfect May morning.

On the crest of a low hill, where a line of larches stood sentinel, Christie spied the open gateway marked on the pencilled sketch-map. Here it was: the private lane leading down to Mr Galvan's lair.

Nervousness formed a dry lump in her throat. Three weeks had gone by since she last saw her patient.

Nursing Tom Galvan in his own home was going to prove a very different matter from having him safely ensconced on Nazareth with the back-up of an entire medical team. 'Any problems — you phone me,' the amiable Sir Frank had reassured her. 'No need to be afraid. Any time, day or night. I'll come galloping down like the Fifth Cavalry —

'Should be plain sailing now, though. You two have been getting on like a house on fire.'

This was gross exaggeration, and Christie knew it, but respectfully forbore from saying so.

The lane spiralled dizzily down and all her concentration was needed in watching out for what lay around the next corner. Wild primroses gleamed like pale stars from amongst the dark ivy wreathing the steep banks. The hazel hedgerows were a tender glowing green. It was like some mysterious journey into another world.

How on earth, marvelled Christie, foot hovering over the brake, does Tom get out of this place in an emergency?

Then suddenly the vista opened out and a slate-roofed cottage came into view, apparently miles from anywhere, set against a backdrop of low green hills.

And there, not a hundred yards beyond, nestling snug into the hollow, lay the spread of a sizeable medieval manor house. Christie idled for a moment on the dusty rutted track and stared down in surprise. Could a neurosurgeon afford *this?*

Gentle May sunshine bathed the ancient stone with a glowing golden wash. Nothing stirred save the gentle breeze in the elms. Not a soul was about, but near a side door sheltering beneath a wooden porch an empty milk crate and a modern plastic dustbin brought the twentieth century to this timeless place. Christie worked out that the house faced down the valley and that she was looking at it from the side. A high wall of the same creamy stone butted on to the building, enclosing what Christie took to be the manor's private grounds. Several dilapidated farm buildings mouldered outside the walls, and the potholed lane led on between tall hedgerows towards distant fields.

She came to an open wrought-iron gateway and steered Matilda on to a gravel track which bordered grassy paddocks running right up to the walls of the manor house. No sign of life here either. The only noise came from birds in the orchard beyond and bees humming round the white-blossomed cherry trees near the barns. There was a smell of sun and blossom and warm new-mown grass.

Christie climbed from the car, leaving the door open, and saw she was in paradise.

For several seconds she stood with her eyes closed, deeply inhaling the sweet refreshing air, her head thrown back to face the sun, almost dizzy with the assault upon her senses, the immense peace and the sense that she had stepped way back in time.

Deep mullioned windows stared down upon her as in a spell she walked up the stone path to the arched medieval porch. Inside it was dark and cool, and to her surprise Christie found the great oak door ajar — as if someone expected her and had left the door open in welcome. Across a flagstoned entrance hall with a beautifully carved screen to one side and a stone wall with two doorways on the right, she could see a patch of sunshine leading out through an identical arched door-way to more grounds behind the house.

Not liking to enter uninvited, she reached out a hand for the iron bellpull on the wall — and at that moment there was movement in the doorway opposite and Tom Galvan appeared in silhouette against the light. 'I thought I heard a car,' came his familiar deep-brown voice. 'Gertie! Hello! You found us all right.'

As he moved towards her — a black outline surrounded by a rim of fire — Christie felt her heart start to pound like a teenager's. She glanced away and back to Matilda gleaming in the sunlight and shivered in the chill shadows as Tom came striding across the flagstones. 'It's good to see you,' he murmured softly, reaching down to kiss her as if she were a guest and not arriving with a job of work to do. He was concerned to put her at her ease, and Christie appreciated that, continuing to feel the pressure of his mouth against her cheek long after the moment was past.

'So you've been rather ill, Gertie.' Tom's expression was genuinely sorry as he examined her face in the half light. 'Well, *I*'ve had all the holiday I'm going to need, so now it's my turn to look after you. Come into the daylight so I can look at you properly.' Dropping a casual arm across her shoulders, he guided her out into the sunshine.

Christie caught her breath at the sight of him. 'Goodness, you're brown!'

'And you look white as a sheet, Gertie. Have to do something about that. You're not intending to wear uniform, I hope, while you're here.' It was a statement rather than a question.

'No, Mr Galvan. I discussed it with Sister and she said it wouldn't be appropriate.' Selfconsciously she smoothed down her narrow black skirt and tugged at the hem of her loose black cotton jersey top. Her black ballerina shoes made her seem tiny

226

against Tom's towering height. She glanced at him again and again from beneath her lashes, mesmerised by the reality of him after three weeks of living on memories.

'So why are you in mourning? Has someone died?'

Christie recovered her poise on a rush of indignation. 'I often wear black, Mr Galvan.' She had packed her case with clothes in suitably dark colours: efficient and unobtrusive wear for private nursing.

By contrast her patient was heart-stoppingly informal. She had never seen Mr Galvan quite like this before.

Around the hospital he looked the dashing doctor in his starched white coats, the eminent consultant in suave dark suits, the formidable surgeon striding purposefully down the ward in his theatre greens. She'd seen him in bed — in his bath — wrapped in a towel — prowling Room 27 in his plaid dressing gown and a variety of moods. Now he was relaxed and welcoming, master of his house. More disturbingly physical than ever. A powerful length of leg on view in well-washed dove grey shorts and trodden-down white espadrilles; open-necked white shirt revealing a Riviera-bronzed and hairy chest.

Of course he had the sort of olive-toned skin that darkened without effort in the sun. His teeth gleamed white and strands of silver sparkled in his thick black wavy hair.

Christie felt suddenly and unac-countably shy — which was ridiculous when she looked back over the many hours and intimate circumstances they had been obliged to share. Once again she encountered Tom's disturbing talent for arousing a selfconsciousness foreign to her nature. Her fingers played with the wooden buckle secur-ing her freshly-shampooed hair neatly at the nape of her neck, and her troubled eyes dwelled on the plaster cast which was the cause of all her disquiet.

She unlocked the boot of her Metro and Tom swung her suitcase out with his good right hand. 'Is this all?' he exclaimed in surprise. 'Surely a girl like you must have plenty of clothes? I was looking forward to seeing you in your glad rags, Gertie.'

Christie tossed her head. 'From now on, Mr Galvan, I shall remain dumb unless you call me Christie,' she challenged. 'Let's start as we mean to go on.'

Tom's laughter rang out over the paddock. He slapped his chest with an open hand. 'Me Tom! You — Christie. Now I'm going to take you up to your room and you can put some shorts on and come and sit with me by the swimming pool. I feel like a swim.' He glanced down at his plaster cast. 'And it's your job to stop me.'

Here we go! Christie tried not look as anxious as she was feeling. 'I ought to take your blood pressure first and check you over,' she said, following Tom inside, carrying a canvas grip and her shoulder bag.

'Plenty of time for that.' His tone brooked no argument and Christie knew she'd have to give in. For the time being — till she found her feet and organised herself and her routine.

Carved ceilings drew her eyes upward as they crossed the lower hall and she almost bumped into Tom as he unlatched a wooden door and paused to let her go first up the winding turret stairs. 'There's not much room to manoeuvre. You'd better go first — I have to proceed with caution.'

Christie could see what he meant. The stone steps were worn and slippery with the traffic of time and you had to clutch on to the rope handrail for safety. Tom with her case hadn't a hand free to steady himself.

'I wish you'd let me take that,' she protested vainly.

'Go on,' encouraged Tom, enjoying the view of her legs in the short tight skirt. 'This is your private staircase. It leads only to your bedroom and bathroom. Look, do go on — you can explore later.'

'Sorry,' she apologised, realising Tom was trying to balance uncomfortably on stairs too worn to accommodate a man-size foot — while she lingered, exclaiming over crimson rhododendrons glimpsed through narrow slitted windows carved out of the massive circular walls. 'It's like living in a castle!' she marvelled, turning round to smile happily at Tom grunting behind her.

'This is the oldest wing of the house, built in the 1470s. The place is an L shape. The rest, if you're interested, is Elizabethan.'

'Oh, I'm interested all right. I get a shiver down my spine just imagining the *history* of a place like this.' They had come to a door and Tom nodded for her to enter.

Christie was lost for words. She could never have pictured herself living and sleeping in the sort of rooms that would not have been out of place in National

Trust properties. 'I feel as if I've stepped back in time for hundreds of years,' she whispered to herself, standing in the centre of the room and turning in a slow circle, her head tilted back, her hair falling to her waist . . .

Walls of oak panelling and on the lofty ceiling the carefully preserved remains of a painted floral design in flaking greens, browns and cream. Stone walls so thick you could curl up with a book in the deep windowsill. Faded rugs flung over waxed floorboards. Simple dark pieces of furniture and a plump paisley eiderdown to match the curtains on the half-tester bed.

'Bathroom's through there,' said Tom casually, but his eagle eyes never left the girl's enthralled face. 'And that door in the panelling leads to my room. Just in case I'm ill in the night, Nurse Gertie! It doesn't lock, I'm afraid, but you can put a chair against it if you're nervous.'

'What door?' queried Christie,

puzzled, running her fingers over the panelling.

Tom showed her. 'It's very low — I have to mind my head. I've had some nasty cracks from that.'

His casual warning brought Christie down to earth again. Of all the many bedrooms there must be in a place this size, what a very convenient arrangement for accommodating girl-friends. A private nurse, of course, didn't come into this category. It would only be sensible to put her within calling distance.

In vain Christie sniffed the air for lingering traces of Diana's lovely perfume. You're pathetically naïve! scoffed an inner voice. She sleeps in Tom's room. She's no shrinking violet. And a man like that . . .

It was uncannily as though Tom could read her thoughts — reaching out to open the connecting door. 'I've got this lovely old four-poster bed. Come and take a look.'

Christie flung a hand out to delay

him. 'Er — later, perhaps. I really should like to unpack before my things get too creased.'

'Of course. I'll be out by the pool. Join me when you're ready.'

When she was alone she opened her small suitcase and pulled a face at its contents. What an uninspiring collection! Dull, unadventurous stuff — Tom wouldn't give her a second glance in this lot.

Rummaging at the bottom of the case among her glamorous silken undies she found what she was looking for, wrapped for safe keeping in a peach crêpe-de-Chine nightdress. She set the silver frame on the table beside her bed, and in this unfamiliar setting Ben's face startled her afresh in its resemblance to his father. Yet Christie could see herself in the child too; Olwen was right.

Someone had lined the drawers of the dark wood chest with delicately rose-perfumed paper. Too good for this lot! thought Christie, dumping her clothes inside and banging the drawers shut in a little flare of temper. She felt very alive, very self-aware. And that was dangerous, because there was only one reason for it.

Pull yourself together, RGN Wisdom! warned her conscience. This man is not available — and neither are you. You *promised* it was just a crush and that you could handle yourself and this job. You had no right to come here otherwise. That's why you chose the clothes, remember? So you'd look like a nurse and not a lovesick idiot.

'For two pins I'd heap the lot in the grate and set a match to them!'

The sunshine outside with its promise of the long hot summer ahead roused such a yearning for the colours of the rainbow and cool gauzy fabrics. She hadn't felt this way for . . . oh, so long.

Fortunately, natural common sense overcame this rash emotional episode and five minutes later she ventured down the turret stairs. It had not occurred to her to pack a bikini or shorts, and anyway it would not do to let Tom realise that secretly she longed to please him — and that her apparent contrariness was her only defence against herself. Since it was unusually warm she had swopped her black top for her least severe white lawn shirt, the short sleeves and low round collar edged with a pleated frill. And she'd removed her cream tights because they seemed a bit formal for lounging in a deckchair by a swimming pool.

'Ne'er cast a clout till May is out,' she reminded herself as with a shiver she crossed the high-vaulted hall with its great fireplace and long refectory table. 'What a perfect place for a candlelit banquet!' she told the silent ghosts haunting the shadows, peeping back over her shoulder as she reached the safety of the sunlit doorway.

Several striped deckchairs were grouped on the new-mown grass, and beside them a tray with a green-and-cream patterned Ironstone coffee pot and matching crockery.

Tom put down his papers and stood up to greet her as, feeling strangely awkward, Christie faked a passing interest in inspecting a huge rhododendron crammed with masses of bursting purply buds.

'You don't look dressed for a swim,' he chided, hooded eyes ranging over her. 'Here I was, hoping you'd be wearing your black bikini.'

This was the old teasing Tom — not some arrogant lord of the manor greeting a new employee.

Instantly Christie found herself relaxing. A half-smile playing about her lips, she regarded Tom's ageing plaster cast and the neglected 'pool'. His shirt lay discarded on the grass. His tan was clearly all-over dark and even.

She sank into the deckchair he indicated. 'I guessed you were pulling my leg, Mr Galvan. See how well I'm getting to know the way your mind works?'

His reply was disturbing in a way she hadn't anticipated. 'That, my dear

Gertie, is because we are tuned to the same wavelength.'

The clear implication was that he had access to her most intimate thoughts! Christie dropped her long lashes and prayed Tom was bluffing and entirely unaware of her surge of pleasure at being with him once more. Control yourself! chided her conscience. Nurses ought not to be disturbed by the sight of tanned and tantalising masculinity within arm's length.

'Your room okay?'

'Perfect!' She tilted her head back, closed her eyes, and let the sun play over her winter-pale skin. There was a rattle of coffee cups.

'No sugar and two pieces of flapjack. To fatten you up.'

He thinks I'm too skinny! 'Thank you,' murmured Christie, conscious of her skirt riding up over her thighs.

'You're being very polite about my swimming pool. The goldfish think it's better than the Caribbean. And there's hundreds of frogs. You do like frogs, don't you?'

Basically Christie was a town girl. She tried hard to feel positive about Tom's frogs, but her toes curled.

'My grandmother had the swimming pool put in — oh, it must have been twenty years ago. She got hold of this vain idea it might keep George and me out of mischief when we were home from boarding school. This was after our parents were killed . . . But a swimming pool's a hell of nuisance to look after. Too much for dear old Stan. The waterlilies lend a nice touch, don't you think? Stan's idea . . . That's him, that little speck in the distance, spraying the apple trees in the orchard. My general factotum and right-hand man is Stan.'

'Ah yes,' said Christie politely, chewing deliciously buttery flapjack and wondering what a brother of Tom's would be like and if he too was a doctor. She pictured the schoolboy Tom. Just the sort of son she hoped she'd be lucky enough to have one day, with scabby sturdy knees and a good-natured charm to match his mischievous eye. Not that Tom's legs deserved that description now — no grazes on those strong brown legs sprawling alongside her slender white ones. A hundred questions hovered on her lips, but she didn't wish to seem nosey about Tom's personal circumstances.

'I used to imagine my own children enjoying this pool. But Diana tells me no one in their right mind would attempt to raise a family here.'

Diana's actual words had been more forthright. 'Listen, Tom, I'm not Miriam Stoppard. I can't make jam and bring up half a dozen kids and appear on TV. Just being on television is hard enough. And the Manor's no place for bringing up children. It's too big — too spooky. Too far from playgroups and kindergartens and shops. The place is a white elephant, Tom. If you sold up, you and George would be laughing all the way to the bank. It's just the place for an Arab or a pop star.'

A brilliant idea struck Christie, the perfect solution to the problem of the house's future. 'If your brother shared it with you . . . two families, I mean. One in the medieval wing and the other in the Elizabethan end.'

Tom smiled at her enthusiasm but shook his head. 'George has sea-water instead of blood in his veins. He could never live inland.'

That answered that question. George must be a sailor.

'My brother designs ships — he's a naval architect.'

There was one piece of flapjack left. 'Please take it. I ate far too much in France.'

Christie stared into the dark weedy waters of the pool where once the young Tom and his brother had played.

'Your fiancée must have enjoyed the break from television,' she commented politely, adding with a sidelong glance at the grounded surgeon, 'I remember you saying she was a workaholic. I thought you a well matched pair.'

At the words 'your fiancée' Tom's expression had darkened. Nervously wondering if she'd spoken out of turn, Christie played with the buckle clasping back her hair.

Tom sprang up from his deckchair and strode the few feet to the edge of the pool. To Christie's alarm he seemed to sway towards the dark green murk shifting gently below him. She feared for his balance and came to stand beside him, linking her arm through his good one with a nurse's concern for her patient. What had she said? What had she done?

Tom stared across the pool to where the lawn ended in a low wall fronted by a hedge of spring-green beeches, looking out over the meadow land beyond. 'I'll be thirty-four this year. Time for a man to marry and settle down.'

He seemed to be speaking to himself, but Christie clung on to him silently.

She felt the fingers of his left hand close over her own. What private misery could such an innocently intended remark have triggered in his mind? She'd mentioned his work ... and Diana ...

It was inconceivable, impossible — the idea of any woman in her right mind rejecting Tom Galvan. But had the impossible nonetheless happened?

Had the television doctor turned her neuro-surgeon down?

8

In a mood that was a complicated mix of frustration and self-doubt, and had nothing to do with Dr Diamond or any other woman, Tom strode into his oak-panelled study and slammed the door on the rest of the world.

Though he was unable to operate, he could still usefully immerse himself in his own investigations into the human pineal. Why should it be that this gland, occupying roughly just one per cent of the human brain, appeared to be vital to man's sense of direction? A third eye in the brain — that was how Descartes, French philosopher and mathematician, had once so aptly described the pineal. If the gland was not functioning, men lost their way.

And here am I, mused Tom, three centuries later, and one among many doctor-detectives *still* trying to solve the pineal mystery.

From his music collection he chose something to match his mood — Amfortas's Lament from *Parsifal*. Righthanded he loaded the compact disc, then went back to settle himself at his desk before pressing the remote control button and allowing the rich melodious baritone of José Van Dam to fill every inch of airspace. Amfortas, wounded by the Holy Spear, lamenting his suffering and begging release . . .

Tom stared sightlessly at the papers spread before him. Could it be that his mind as well as his body had been damaged in the accident? Had that steely nerve at last deserted him? Supposing the arm healed one hundred per cent, as Jonathan so confidently predicted; was the mind going to prevent him ever taking up his scalpel again?

The telephone buzzed. Tom pressed the remote control and abruptly cut

Amfortas short. 'Yes?' he growled unhelpfully. 'Oh, it's you, Frank. How am I? Still the dark night of the soul . . .

'I *know* you warned me this is how it would be. Because I was so badly injured I've experienced a body-image disturbance. The damn plaster cast is temporarily alienating me from myself. And for this reason I'm now experiencing a lack of confidence in my damaged arm and hand. Once the cast's removed and I get back in the saddle, etcetera, etcetera.

'Yes, she's arrived. Out of uniform, of course! What did you expect? Looking very efficient and proper, though. I pulled her leg a bit — told her she looked as if she might be clinically depressed. What! . . . You rather think she *has* been in the past . . . ?

'Of course I'm still here. That would be very pleasant. Actually it's my birthday.'

Frank's chuckle rolled down the line. 'That little whizz of a secretary of yours reminded me. Give you three guesses who the hostess will be!'

A few minutes later came a knock at the door. Tom pushed the diary aside and shouted 'Enter!' as his third finger touched the control button.

A blast of plaintive baritone hit Christie as she carried in her patient's lunch on a tray. She recognised the music immediately: Wagner.

Her father had often listened to the Lament when one of his theatrical projects wasn't going well. The fact that Tom was playing it now was indicative of his state of mind. He was clearly sorrowing over Diana Diamond — and all Christie's tender loving care was powerless to ease his special pain.

In a rattle of cutlery the tray landed on Tom's desk and Christie, her hands shaking, bolted for the door.

'You eating with Bess?'

Conscious of curious eyes boring into her retreating back, she nodded but did not turn around.

'Come back in half an hour and we'll go through the diary.'

* * *

For lunch Bess had produced bowls of delicious Irish stew and crusty bread still hot from the oven. Seated on a wheelback chair at the scrubbed kitchen table, Christie could not help but appreciate the good food and comforts of an up-to-date kitchen housed in an historic home.

The Manor's original stone-floored kitchen with its pantries and sculleries had been preserved by Eleanor Galvan as a testament to the house's history. They formed the central point of the ground floor, right next to the medieval dining hall: a cool and echoey whitewashed thoroughfare for people crossing from one wing to the other.

A modern kitchen had been installed at the far end of the Tudor section, across the passage from the old lady's pleasant sitting room. Sunshine spilled through French windows on to saggy armchairs with faded blue covers, mellowing the hues of Oriental rugs on golden-waxed floors. She had been particularly fond of the view across the garden to the pool and the meadow beyond, Tom had recalled. Ruefully he pointed out shelves of novels, and an old black-and-white television, covered with a dustcloth, on a Jacobean table with barley sugar twist legs.

His grandmother's favourite room, said Tom, and Christie must have sole use of it during her stay. He wanted to replace the television, and buy in a selection of up-to-date paperbacks, but Christie said she wouldn't hear of it. Old books were fascinating; and if she needed entertainment, she murmured tongue-in-cheek, she'd listen to Tom's records through the study wall.

'It's a good job Tom doesn't have neighbours,' she observed dryly, the good food quite restoring her despondent spirits.

Bess chuckled. She was a stout country body with long once-red hair fixed back with tortoiseshell hairpins in a wispy pepper-and-salt bun. 'Only me and Stan up the lane in our cottage. Grand opera — that's what Mr Tom likes best. He never bothers with the TV, just plays his gramophone till all hours. Are you a fan of the opera too, then, Nurse Wisdom?'

'I've hardly listened to any serious music over the last few years.'

It was an evasive answer, and Christie changed the subject to the far more interesting one of Tom Galvan and his extraordinary home; and the caretakers themselves, who turned out not to be the native village couple she had taken them for.

She learned that Stan was in fact Stanislaus Capek, and that he had escaped from Czechoslovakia when Hitler's troops invaded. Seeking refuge in Britain, the tall thin young man with the gentle eyes had been befriended by Bess's older brother. And when the telegram came from the War Office, regretting that Bess's young husband had been killed leaving her a widow with a tiny daughter, Stan had been the one to comfort her with his long-concealed love. 'He found work as caretaker in the village school, not a mile down yon lane. And I ended up as head cook — aye, I did! — when our three girls got older.' There was a faraway look in the tired blue eyes. Bess clearly made no distinction in her mind between her first child and Stan's two babies.

'Gracious, I assumed the lane just ran on into fields.'

'Bless you, dear, you came what we call the scenic route.' Bess threw up her hands in amusement. 'Mr Tom would never get to the hospital if yon was the only way out! Well, as I was saying, in time they closed the village school and me and Stan had the good fortune to be taken on at the Manor by old Mrs Galvan. Mind you, we weren't no spring chickens ourselves. And we're not getting any younger, see.'

Oh dear! thought Christie. Whatever would Tom do without the Capeks? But Stan's beard was grizzled and his hands gnarled with arthritis, his once-straight back beginning to stoop with age.

'We've been thinking. A little place in Lyme, near Margarete, our youngest, would suit us fine.' Bess dried her hands on her apron and offered Christie a bowl of fruit.

'Thanks, Mrs Capek.' She selected a banana and peeled it thoughtfully. Poor Tom! yet another problem for his broad shoulders to bear. There had been no indication that he was aware of such plans in their earlier conversation.

'Have you mentioned this to Mr Galvan?' It would come as a blow, no doubt about that; a couple such as the Capeks would be mighty difficult to replace. Yet Tom himself must be well aware that it was a lot of work for an elderly couple.

Bess poured coffee for Mr Tom and his nurse, preferring a pot of tea for herself and Stan who would be coming up to the house for his dinner in half an hour. 'We're biding our time, m'dear,' she explained, lowering her voice

— though Tom would have required a bionic ear to hear one word through the intensity of sound vibrating the study walls.

'We wouldn't want to worry him when he's been so ill. You won't say anything, Nurse, will you?'

Bess dried her hands on a clean towel, then, on an impulse to confide, pulled another wheelback chair closer to this young nurse who was so very different from the alarming Dr Diamond. 'We reckon Dr Diamond'll get her way in the end. She'd have Mr Tom sell up and go to one of them London hospitals.' She patted Christie's arm reassuringly. 'Me and Stan can hold on till then. Till he marries and goes to London. So don't you be worryin', Nurse.'

While Mrs Capek took Tom's coffee to the study, Christie sat brooding over this shattering news. Sell the Manor. Quit Joe's. Marry Diana and live in London because all of this suited the TV doctor!

The prospect of Joe's without its hero was too awful to contemplate.

Yet by the sound of it, the plans were made and had only to be finalised. Two such busy people — just a question of agreeing upon a convenient date, once Tom had been pronounced one hundred per cent fit again and ready to resume work. How foolish of me to imagine there could be anything wrong between such a charismatic pair, Christie chided herself.

Suddenly the music ceased. 'Christie!'

She gulped her coffee and automatically her hands went to check the angle of a non-existent cap. Still smiling at her mistake, she walked into the study to find Tom with his back to her, a red lambswool sweater slung across his shoulders, staring out through the diamond leads at the sunny lane beyond. The room now seemed forbiddingly dark without its colourful sound. The book-lined walls absorbed the small north light. It was a wonder Tom could see to work. 'You wanted to go through your diary with me,' she reminded him, 'to review the week ahead. And what about the documents I'm to start translating?'

As he slowly turned, Christie was startled to discover herself facing a stern, forbidding stranger in heavy black-framed spectacles. 'Oh! I didn't know you wore — ' she exclaimed involuntarily.

He drew them off, rubbed his eyes and forehead with his left hand, the old Tom once more. 'I never seem to see you wearing yours these days.'

'Mine? I don't wear gl- . . . oh, those,' she finished lamely.

'All the better to keep your eye on the wolf, eh, Nurse?' Tom flipped open the diary. Christie's mouth was tight at the edges. One mistake and you were never allowed to forget it.

'Two-thirty tomorrow, a meeting here with the senior members of my firm. Would you be prepared to sit in and make notes for us?'

She folded her arms, shivering in the

thin blouse as the sunless room struck chill. 'I haven't any shorthand, but I'm perfectly happy to make myself useful in any way.'

Tom raised a meaningful eyebrow. 'Is that a promise, young woman?'

Christie stared him out for three whole seconds, then gave in and blushed. Tom's wondrous grin would have melted an iceberg. She just knew she'd see that look tonight in her dreams.

'Better wear your specs and do your hair in that frigid super-nurse style. I don't want Kingsley seeing how beautiful you really are. He's after a wife to go with a consultant's post. Married candidates tend to be preferred. I'd offer him Diana — but these days she tends to scare the pants off men.'

Christie wasn't sure whether it was shiver or shock that made her teeth rattle audibly and gooseflesh break out beneath her clenched fingers. But she'd just learned three things she didn't know before. That hospital appointments committees preferred their consultants safely wed. That the gentlemanly Mr. Galvan could without batting an eyelid crack a joke that was in extremely questionable taste. And that he considered her . . . beautiful.

This final point was too fascinating, too *dangerous* to contemplate in his presence. With extreme effort Christie drove it to the back of her mind. Dry-throated, she stammered out, 'B-b-but you're a consultant and you're not married!' It wasn't a very sensible remark, but she could hardly just stand there in quivering silence.

Taking his time about it, Tom looked her over quizzically, examining the girl from under heavy speculative lids. Was it cold in his study? He rarely felt the cold. But Christie seemed all of a tremble.

He pulled off his scarlet sweater and came to stand in front of her, clumsily wrapping its warmth around her shoulders and looping the sleeves so they dangled over her blouse buttons. A hand resting on her shoulder, he murmured jokingly in response to that impromptu protest, 'Look at the havoc I've wreaked at Joseph's. Bleeding hearts in the nurses' home, swoons in the corridors as I pass by, fumbling fingers in theatre. Of course the powers-that-be prefer married men. It makes for a quieter life all round.

'Tell you what, Gertie, you can marry me if you like. I've grown accustomed to your face. Promise me you won't run off with Kingsley Armstrong tomorrow.'

More of Tom's tasteless joking! Christie longed to puncture his levity with a challenging eye and the dignified, if Victorian, declaration, 'Mr Galvan, I would have you know I am engaged to Dr James Mallory.' But she couldn't say it because it wasn't true. So instead she just stepped back out of his grasp, looked as coolly unperturbed as she could manage, and said, 'Who is this Gertie, Mr Galvan? Next item in your diary, please.'

'Wednesday. A meeting at the Royal College of Surgeons. Can you drive me to the station and meet the six-thirty train? Good, I'll pay your petrol, of course. Then Saturday night — dinner with Sir Frank Davy.'

Christie frowned. She didn't mind in the least ferrying Tom from A to B and she certainly wouldn't take money for the petrol. But if it meant the chauffeuse must be tolerated at Sir Frank's dinner table . . . 'I should really rather not, Mr Galvan.'

He looked distinctly annoyed. 'Well, you can retire to the local hostelry if you prefer. But Frank will be hurt and disappointed at your refusal to accept an invitation extended as much to you as to myself.'

There was a coldness in his voice which Christie had never noticed before.

'I'm sorry.' She spoke quietly, her head held high. 'I didn't mean to be ungracious. I only thought it wasn't my place — '

Tom's exasperated eyebrows silenced her attempt to explain. 'We're not living in the Middle Ages, woman! You may be here under my roof for a few weeks, but you are not my servant and I'm not your master . . . Good God! You never showed me much deference when I was laid up in hospital — I shall be highly disappointed if you start doing so now!'

Christie covered her mouth with a tactful hand, but her eyes gave her away. And this verbal skirmish ended in mutual and good-natured laughter.

★ ★ ★

James telephoned that evening to make sure she had arrived safely, interrupting the cold meat and salad supper, left ready in the pantry by Bess Capek, which nurse and patient were sharing companionably in the kitchen. Tom had been describing some interesting neuro-surgical cases when the phone in the sitting room shrilled its call and he answered.

'For you. Dr James Mallory.'

When she returned, Tom found

himself looking for telltale signs indicating the condition of Nurse Wisdom's heart. But Christie, so far as he could tell, remained her calm, uncomplicated self. If the sound of her lover's voice made her pulses race and her heart beat faster, then it was well concealed from prying eyes. She might have been speaking to Directory Enquiries for all the emotion her private conversation seemed to have generated. Tom smiled to himself with a certain wry satisfaction.

Unaware of Tom's speculations concerning her romance with Dr Mallory, Christie picked up her knife and fork and resumed her supper with all the gusto of an effortlessly slim lass with a healthy appetite. 'Gosh, but it's wonderful to tuck into a plate of meat again! James'll never succeed in making a true vegetarian of me. Mmm. You know something, Tom? Your Mrs Capek is a treasure.'

Tom's fork was chasing an awkward slice of gammon round his plate. He was fed up with having his food cut up for him like a three-year old. 'Do you like cooking?'

'Absolutely love it. I expect that's because I'd never even boiled an egg till I was a student nurse.' Tom was about to enquire why, but she chatted on, 'James is staying at the cottage and keeping an eye on the place while I'm working here. The only problem seems likely to be his old car refusing to start in the mornings. He's used to walking to work. His flat is only round the corner from Joe's.'

Tom jabbed viciously at a slippery piece of tomato. 'So you two don't live together.'

He didn't sound a bit surprised. He even looked mildly approving when Christie's answer came pat and prim and prudish. 'No, we do not.'

'Think what you'd save on the rent.'

'I own the cottage,' said Christie coldly. 'If Dr Mallory wished to move in with me permanently I should be perfectly happy for him to do so.'

Tom pulled a face and seemed uninterested. 'Good for you.' But he was puzzled all the same. Young Gertie here actually *owned* her own place, drove round town in a brand new Mini Metro — and possessed a wardrobe of clothes that suggested she was happier in her nursing uniform. Her pathologist boy-friend, on the other hand, lived in a seedy flat, and drove an unreliable old banger that wouldn't start in the mornings.

Unusual indeed — especially since nurses' pay was abysmal. Tom uttered a hollow laugh and tossed back his glass of wine. Maybe Mallory was after Gertie's money!

He topped up her wine glass and refilled his own, recalling how Frank Davy had hinted that Wisdom suffered from — correction, *had* suffered from — depression . . .

He drained that glass too, then finished off the bottle of Rioja, telling himself that with every passing day the intriguing Staff Nurse Wisdom grew ever more mysterious and fascinating.

To think, he brooded, when I first saw her that night in the car park I took her for a carefree, uncomplicated young woman! What a grandfather of a mistake.

He put the million-dollar question: the one expecting the affirmative answer. 'Are you and Dr Mallory engaged?'

With a little shrug of her shoulders Christie said no, they were not. She was surprised that the words came so easily when but a short while ago she'd been so anxious to marry the solid and dependable James Mallory. Perhaps after all her pathologist wasn't Mr Right. Mr Right might be more like Tom Galvan, drawing her to him like a magnet, his teasing dark eyes and his smile arousing in her the oddest mix of emotions, and far too physical and energetic and forceful ever to be safe and dependable and boring. But then Tom Galvan in waking hours was her patient. Only in dreams dared her subconscious acknowledge him as a lover . . . her Mr Impossible.

★ ★ ★

Christie had slipped quietly into a chair at the back of the study, placing herself at the rear of the group since she was only attending to take down dictation.

Mr Armstrong, Tom's senior registrar, had arrived in a two-seater open-topped sports car with Dr Guiles, the anaesthetist. The others had followed, squashed into Sister Calloway's white Fiesta.

The sky was overcast and the study lamps had been switched on.

They were discussing numbers of beds and discharges of various patients, and Kingsley Armstrong was doing a lot of talking which no one seemed to want recorded for posterity. Christie's mind had lately discovered a disquieting tendency to veer off at a tangent . . .

She recalled how comfortable the

bed had been, and how she'd slept like a top, out for the count the moment her head hit the pillow. No dreams. No nightmares. And no lying awake thinking of Tom in his four-poster only yards away!

After supper she had washed the dishes and tidied the kitchen. She wandered through the grounds for half an hour and gasped with delight to see a magnificent white owl fly silent-winged out of one of the barns. Then she'd spent half an hour in the sitting room, trying vainly to read and eventually giving up the attempt to control her wayward thoughts.

On her way to bed, she had called goodnight round the study door. But Tom was deep in concentration and apart from a vague reply hardly seemed aware she was there. Very likely he had stayed up half the night, working. Christie supposed she should have insisted on a sensible bedtime for her convalescent patient; but on day one it seemed tactful to ease oneself in with the minimum of fuss . . .

Surrounded by his surgical team, this was Tom in an entirely new light: no longer the injured patient, but the boss man in action. There was an atmosphere in the room and an aura about Tom: the powerful and confident aura that surrounds any professional man at the peak of his physical and intellectual powers.

As head of neuro-surgery he had built up a tremendous reputation for himself and the work of his department.

But Tom refused to play the rôle of doctor-god. For the most part his manner was easy and affable as he approved and organised and delegated. And his surgical team responded with an energy and vigour that Christie found very exciting to listen to. Clearly they were all raring to have him back at the helm.

'Make a note of that, please.' Tom's eyes were trained on her daydreaming face. He repeated the name of the patient whose brain scan they had been discussing. 'To be admitted for treatment with steroids to reduce swelling around the tumour.'

He turned to Kingsley and advised, 'You'll have to get in there fast and unplug the drainage system. As soon as he's strong enough, I want to excise that tumour myself.'

Faces brightened at this confirmation that Mr Galvan's grave injuries were almost healed; and only Tom knew what it had cost him to make that commitment — to a patient whose life now depended upon a neuro-surgeon's courage.

But Christie, with a flicker of anxiety, noted the inner tension sharpening the planes and contours of his sombre, handsome face. A lump rose in her throat and along with it a rush of immoderate love for this man that almost threatened to overwhelm her.

A set of X-rays had been produced and the team were discussing a spinal cord injury due for surgery. It was decided that the Senior Registrar would operate with the SHO assisting. 'How did it happen?' enquired the Theatre Sister.

'She fell out of a tree and cracked her spine.' Using a black felt-tip pen, Tom sketched a diagram of the spinal cord and marked on it the area of lesion, pointing out the nerves involved. Glancing at her watch, Christie saw it was time to warn Bess that in ten minutes they would be ready for tea, served buffet-style on the refectory table of the dining hall. Unobtrusively she slipped out to lend a hand.

★ ★ ★

Some of the group had not visited the house before and were bombarding their host with questions concerning its past history. He promised everyone a guided tour after they had made the most of Bess's spread of egg-and-cress sandwiches, farm-buttered drop scones, her rich plum cake and featherlight coffee sponge.

Mr Armstrong made a beeline for Christie and grasping her elbow drew her out of earshot and into a shadowy corner by the linenfold screen. She couldn't resist glancing back over her shoulder in search of Tom's eye: and sure enough his lazy half-smile warned she'd get her leg pulled later.

Mr Armstrong was a nice-looking man, only a year or so younger than Tom — but in complete physical contrast, being small and wiry with curly fair hair and shrewd blue eyes. Christie felt certain he was too preoccupied with his consultant's health to notice whether the nurse had knock knees and a squint. All the same, it sent a tingle down her spine to imagine Tom being jealous.

Good lord! . . . how did I come to overlook this one? Kingsley Armstrong was examining Nurse Wisdom with a covert eye. Her hair was different — swept up above each pearl-studded ear with tortoiseshell combs. He thought how poised and feminine she looked in her grey silk shirt and neat dark skirt with matching shoes and tights. Fabulous legs. But a bit on the tall side for his liking. 'What a relief to see him well on the mend.'

Both their heads turned to study Tom, tanned and healthy, and apparently absorbed in conversation with Dr Guiles over by the huge log fire Stan had prepared that morning.

'Mmm. I feel a fraud being here, but Sir Frank was so insistent. I only agreed because I had some holiday due and this seemed a useful way of using it up. Tom could be overdoing it, though. Working on papers and lectures till all hours. Not much I can do about that.'

Tom, eh? . . . Kingsley admired Nurse Wisdom's innocent wide-eyed expression. He didn't believe a word of that about the boss slaving away till all hours. Though the plaster must spoil their fun a bit.

And good luck to him! mused Kingsley, who couldn't think of a polite term to illustrate his opinion of Diana

Diamond. He polished off his fifth drop scone and to prolong this interesting conversation with the decidedly intriguing Nurse Wisdom, queried, 'Presumably you're keeping on with the usual checks — and making sure he's not . . . um — taking any physical risks?'

'Oh, of course. Though it will be a relief when that plaster comes off and we know for sure that Tom's going to be able to operate again. He gets very frustrated at times.'

'I'll bet. But it's quite difficult for doctors to tell when a fracture is fully healed. Manual examination and X-rays can give ambiguous results. The orthopods won't be in a hurry to take risks with our great man.'

★   ★   ★

The water was warm and caressing, silky with Chanel bath oil and redolent of the sensual fragrance of No 5.

Christie allowed herself a ten-minute soak, then towelled herself dry and brushed out her tangled mass of hair, fixing it back in a heavy ponytail, moist tendrils escaping untidily at the nape of her neck and around her ears. She looked doubtfully at the Benetton denims she'd packed as an after-thought, then decided, why not? I can always change into a skirt after breakfast.

A testament to Mrs Capek's good cooking, the jeans clung close as a second skin. The weather remained comfortably warm, so Christie didn't bother with a bra under her oversized primrose tee-shirt. She slipped her bare toes into a pair of white espadrilles and considered herself ready to begin the first official task of the day.

The hospital had loaned her all the necessary equipment and record charts, stowed into a black leather case. Christie collected this from the bottom of the wardrobe and — disturbingly aware of the mingled tension and pleasurable anticipation which seemed the hallmark of her relationship with this very special patient — lifted her hand to knock (after a second or two's hesitation) upon the door connecting the two bedrooms.

There was no one else about in the whole of the building. Mrs Capek didn't start work until nine. 'Mr Galvan. May I come in?'

9

Tom yawned heavy-eyed among the rumpled splendour of his four-poster, linen sheets hitched carelessly about his middle, rich plum velvet covers tumbling on to the floor. He had discarded such niceties as pyjamas on his escape from Nazareth Wing and the officious — Christie pulled a rueful face — Nurse Wisdom.

'And what time did we get to bed this morning?' she enquired briskly, setting down her case on a sturdy Elizabethan chest before tugging open the heavy oyster brocade curtains. A shaft of morning sunshine illuminated uneven creaky floorboards. The room was far too large to carpet, one rumpled Turkish rug, soft as cloth, spread beside Tom's bed.

'MYOB,' drawled her patient, rousing himself on the pile of pillows that supported his arm, the better to watch as Christie strode round the room tut-tutting and flinging open windows to let in a breath of fresh air.

From her case she produced a thermometer which she stuck in his mouth while she took his pulse. Checked the reading — which was perfectly normal, as expected — and recorded her observations on the morning chart.

'Before I forget,' interrupted Tom, 'there's a German medical journal interested in publishing a couple of my recent neuro-surgical papers. Can you manage an English-to-German translation, do you think?'

It gave Christie a good feeling inside to know he depended upon her in this small way. 'I shall do my best,' she told him modestly, turning aside for a moment to hide the telltale sparkle of pleasure brightening her eyes and removing the sphygmomanometer (on loan from the hospital) from its wooden box.

'And now let's check your BP.' Stethoscope at the ready and with Tom's arm resting on a convenient pillow, she fixed the inflatable rubber cuff firmly and evenly around the hard muscles of his upper arm. Then, her fingers in contact with the radial pulse and her eye on the line of mercury in the manometer, she inflated the cuff and placed the bell of the stethoscope above Tom's inner elbow. A moment or two later it was all over and Tom was crowing over the enviable level of his blood pressure. 'Not bad, eh, for a man who's almost thirty-five! Just wait till this damn plaster comes off and I can get back on the squash court.'

His nurse was playing it cool. 'Mmm, all things considered . . . Let's see how your scar's coming along.' Without waiting for an invitation Christie flipped back the sheets and peered at Tom's incision, healing nicely, the scar tissue healthily pink. 'Now I see why you threw your egg and bacon break-fasts at us! Here we have living proof that the vitamins contained in grapefruit *do* promote wound recovery. Well done, Doctor! Full marks.'

She leaned across to cover his exposed abdomen, smelling faintly delicious, soft tendrils of hair falling with charming but most uncharacteristic untidiness about her face, her bare arms skinny in the loose sleeves of her primrose T-shirt.

Her proximity suddenly jogged Tom's memory! His good hand closed over her wrist, pulling relentlessly until Christie was forced down on the bed beside him. 'Hey! You owe me an explanation, young woman. *I* saw you yesterday, making assignations with my number two. Didn't I warn you about him? ... Mmm, you do smell nice. Don't tell me, let me guess — Chanel No 5? I once had an actress friend who — '

'Ouch!' complained Christie, wriggling in a half-hearted attempt to escape from Tom's grasp, 'I don't know what you're talking about. All Kingsley wanted to know was — stop that at once!' As if it were electrified she jumped off the bed, crimson-faced and wide-eyed with apparent indignation.

'I was right, you're not wearing a bra. How shocking, Nurse Wisdom!'

Christie tugged down her shirt and with jittery hands tried to anchor her disobedient hair. But the rubber band had snapped and a shining wayward mass suddenly poured itself over her shoulders. Tom grinned. This was the very antithesis of the usual severely tidy and composed Nurse Wisdom, swaying before him like a sapling in a breeze, her breathing shocked and ragged, tossing her head like a wild and defiant pony.

The safest thing to do is ignore that jibe! decided Christie, calming herself with a great effort of will. After all, this *is* the nineteen-eighties — and outside St Joseph's I may dress as I please. Tom gets some male chauvinist kick out of trying to make me blush. And idiot that I am, I've fallen for it again.

But for all her determination not to let her heart rule her head, Christie knew she was fighting a losing battle. Her feelings for Tom were running out of control, possessed of a strength and intensity she had never felt for James. And it only added fuel to the flames when Tom behaved like this, teasing her as a woman and not just the nurse he was stuck with . . . even taunting her, in that amiably sardonic manner, with the disturbing revelation that he found her interesting and attractive.

Where was it all going to end?

'That's quite enough of that, Mr Galvan!' she warned, apparently as calm and collected as ever. 'I do hope we're not going to have this palaver *every* morning.'

Later in her room she curled up on the deep window-sill, arms wrapped about her knees, reflecting that Tom Galvan had entered her life in circumstances of high drama; and that since nursing him, sharing a quietly predictable future with the dependable Dr

Mallory had somehow lost its appeal.

She peered down from her high perch upon Stan Capek, trundling a wheelbarrow along the path leading down to the meadow.

'What a corny thing I've done! Fallen head over heels in love with my surgeon-patient, just like the heroines do in romantic fiction. What's going to come of it all?'

The voice of reason came up with the only answer. 'Nothing, Nurse Wisdom. Nothing at all. You'll finish nursing this case and return to St Joseph's to take up your new post. In time, the cautious James — yes, he is cautious, and that's one of the reasons why you value him, because he's never going to precipitate you into unwelcome dramas — in time he will give sensible and well-thought-out reasons why the two of you should get hitched. You will say yes and heave a sigh of relief because that's the future all sewn up, safe and certain. What more could a refugee like you want? Tom will marry Dr Diamond and make a great name for himself at Guy's or the Royal Hanoverian or somewhere equally illustrious. And you'll read about him and his famous wife in the gossip columns and shudder, thanking your lucky stars because after all you managed to escape from that sort of world.

'Yes, but —

'No buts. Your dreams are dangerous — dangerous because neither of you are free of commitments, and a love affair with Tom Galvan will hurt two other very special people. Besides, aren't you reading too much significance into a few teasing remarks?'

Biting her lip, Christie sought refuge in action, springing from her perch and gathering up the dictionary and the papers she'd been working on all afternoon. Hardly sensible, was it, to loll about indulging in emotional fantasies over a man who certainly did not love her — even if he might not kick her out of his bed! That was all it could mean to a bored Tom Galvan, a

282

brief interlude to relieve the tedium of convalescence.

She went to the bathroom and examined the reflection of her pale face and sad eyes. Another and more practical problem loomed on the horizon, and she'd better start thinking of a solution pretty quick.

★　★　★

'One first-class day return to Waterloo,' requested Tom, gripping his briefcase under his right arm and resting his wallet on the ticket office counter. Christie had carefully pinned the empty left sleeve of his jacket so that his arm was quite neatly concealed. The train was in and he strode down the platform, a commandingly tall and distinguished figure in his expensive dark suit, looking for an empty compartment in which to work uninterrupted.

Christie watched her wounded hero disappear inside a first-class carriage, then bought her own second class ticket and found a seat among the crowds at the other end of the train, as far from Mr Galvan as possible. 'Meet me off the six-thirty,' he had ordered. And that would fit in quite nicely with her plans.

At Waterloo Station, from a cautious distance she saw him head for the Underground entrance, then, when she was sure the coast was clear, she bought her own ticket for Marble Arch.

Oxford Street was as hatefully congested as ever and reinforced her dislike of London, now that she no longer had to live there. She stopped at Marks and Spencer to stock up with support stockings for work (better to be safe than sorry) and to buy a packet of prawn sandwiches to eat on the train home, then strolled on till she came to the secretive turning on the left that led the cognoscenti towards St Christopher's Place.

It had been several years since Christie had paid any serious thought to what she wore: now she was surprised to discover how the sight of all these covetable clothes made her heart beat faster as she pictured herself wearing them for Tom. He wanted colour? He should have it. He wanted her to look nice for Sir Frank's dinner party? She'd stun him. He wouldn't recognise Staff Nurse Wisdom.

The whole day stretched ahead. For over an hour she browsed around her old haunts, just window-shopping and admiring the fashionably dressed women parading up and down South Molton Street. Then she started to buy shoes and casual summer wear, secure in the knowledge that there was no shortage of money in the bank, and that her eye for what suited her colouring and tall slenderness was sound as ever.

It must be something special for Sir Frank's dinner party — nothing fussy or overdone, but sophisticated and up to the minute. Tom should see her with fresh eyes. And Sir Frank should not regret a polite invitation extended in kindness to Tom's private nurse.

No doubt about where to find the right dress. Brown's it must be: where once Archie Wisdom's daughter had run up a huge account. They might even remember her, the ex-*Vogue* model . . .

Finally, and now quite laden with colourful bags, Christie headed for Selfridges' Perfume Hall to stock up with Prescriptives cosmetics.

Then the laden struggle back to Waterloo and an earlier train than Tom was to catch. Stow her shopping in the boot, and appear at the station as if she'd just driven from the Manor to collect her VIP patient.

★   ★   ★

'Nurse Wisdom!' Tom rapped a peremptory tattoo on the communicating door between their bedrooms.

'Nurse Wisdom — this is your Lord of the Manor come to claim his rights.' Tom couldn't help chuckling at his own wit. He was in a good mood: the day in town had done him good — fellow surgeons congratulating him on a textbook recovery and saying how great it was to have him back in their midst.

Till the accident he hadn't realised he had so many friends. So many nice people, the world was a wonderful place. His confidence was back. He was over the hump now, he was sure of it, and it was in no small way due to his wonderful Gertie. He'd bought her a present.

Still no reply to his knock. Tom opened the door and poked his head round. 'Christie?' Perhaps she was taking a shower. He called again — no answer. He'd leave the two letters on her bed (funny she hadn't found them, they must have been lying around all day) — the one from Sussex and the Swiss airmail, and hang on to the other thing till later. She was probably down in the kitchen chattering away to Bess.

Tom walked over to the bed and dropped the letters on the eiderdown, looking curiously about him as if he'd never seen the room before. Faintly the scent of her hung upon the air, and the place was as neat as he might have guessed it would be, everything tidied away out of sight. Everything but a limp blue dress dangling from a padded satin hanger against the wardrobe door.

Tom stroked the blue fabric with a thoughtful hand. It felt wonderful: soft as a feather. Hell's teeth, but of course! This was what she was planning to wear: nice colour — but floppy and shapeless and in the best of unadventurous taste.

Thrusting out his bottom lip, Tom considered the package he was carrying, the strapless satin red thing he'd been such an idiot to buy. He could see now how totally unsuitable it was for Frank's do. She'd never have agreed to wear it. He must have been out of his mind.

There was a photo by the bed, a silver-framed portrait of a toddler half smiling, half doubtful of the photographer. The likeness was obvious: Christie herself, perhaps twenty years ago.

Tom examined the photo with a sentimental eye — this was what her own children would look like one day, with cherubic little faces and tousled mops of brown curls. But closer observation showed a pencilled inscription in the left-hand corner, and he realised with a start that this child could not be Christie. In fact it was a boy. And the boy's name was . . . 'Ben' written faintly in Christie's own hand, just above the recent month and year.

Tom straightened, frowning, rubbing his chin with his hand, an unconscious habit when he was puzzled. He knew well enough it was none of his business, but . . . Ben. Ben. Who was this Ben?

A suspicion was taking form in Tom's mind. His expression was that of a man in pain who feared he had stumbled upon a secret he should never have known about. But was this child the solution to the mystery of Christie Wisdom? She must have begun her RGN training at an older age than most girls. Why? Why did she keep herself to herself and avoid the social life of Joe's? He'd never seen her around the place till that night. Such a special girl, with a special dignity and a special pain behind her calm eyes.

She must have had a baby. And Ben was that child.

Tom retreated to his own bedroom and tried to rationalise his own feelings about this discovery. Why was he so upset? What had this to do with himself? Was Christie Wisdom — or had she been? — married? Did she pay someone to look after her child while she worked to maintain the two of them? And if this was so, what could he, Tom Galvan, do to help the nurse to whom he owed a debt beyond gratitude?

Surely she must need money. But her cottage, and her new car? Had they been provided by the father? And Dr Mallory — where did he fit into all this?

Tom sprawled on his bed, staring sightlessly at the velvet lining over his head. He heard Christie's door open and close, but the walls were too solid for him to hear any of her movements as she found her letters and opened them and she too lay down on her bed to read the latest news from her mother and stepmother. She turned to Olwen's first, for news of the child.

'... Don't worry about Ben, the doctor thinks it's just a virus and he'll throw it right off as the weather gets warmer. I've had an awful cold myself. You know what worriers we singers are, always panicking about our throats and swallowing antibiotics. If your technique is good enough you can sing through anything — so they tell us! I hope I shan't have to put that to the test this season. You will come and hear me, won't you, Christie dear ... I do understand your dread of going to an opera, but wouldn't it be healthier to meet the ordeal head-on instead of ducking out? I'll get the Glyndebourne tickets and you bring that lovely Dr Mallory you write of in your letters

. . . *Carmen*'s first performance next week — wish me luck!'

★ ★ ★

Christie was down in the meadow. The ground was quite dry and she lay hidden in the long grasses, staring up at the blue sky.

It was incredibly peaceful: not the trace of a breeze to add its whisper to the birdsong and the chirrup of crickets. So many different wild flowers, she noticed in delight; meadows untouched by chemicals and fertilisers were becoming a rarity in the English landscape.

To her right stretched the old orchard; a hundred yards to her left, concealed by a high stone wall, the lane and the Capeks' delightful cottage. Beyond the orchard, the dank medieval fishpond with its rusting waterwheel disappearing into the depths beside. A dangerous spot for children, though; no wonder Dr

Diamond had her reservations about bringing up a family here!

Such a place as this should be shared by more than a bachelor surgeon and his faithful retainers! sighed Christie with a niggle of resentment that a few should be so privileged. A few years ago the thought would never have occurred to her: but nursing had altered her perspective on life and she found herself growing increasingly concerned for the people she nursed.

Imagining Tom and Diana's children playing hide-and-seek in this very meadow brought the image of little Ben strongly before her eyes. He hadn't been very well last time Olwen wrote. But the latest letter had been redirected by James and was a few days out of date: Ben would be full of beans once more, a handful and no mistake.

Christie kicked off her new white sandals and turned on to her front, resting her chin on sun-warmed arms. Her heavy plait of hair lay heavy on the bare skin of her spine. She'd bought the sundress in Whistles, a clear raspberry pink cotton with an easy dropped waist and buttoned straps which crossed over the low back. A frivolous outfit — but so cool and comfy in the unexpected heat of this glorious May.

When my job's over, she decided, I'll drive down to Sussex, wriggle out of the Glyndebourne invitation and have Ben to myself for two or three days before getting back into hospital routine.

A bumblebee came droning along to settle on a purple clover flower inches from her nose. Town girl that she was, Christie rolled away in mild alarm and with a heartfelt sigh announced into the silence, 'It is hard, you know, to be both mother and father to a child.'

A shadow blacked out the sky and she sat up with a start, shielding her eyes with her arm as the shadow moved and let the sun's rays beat upon her face. 'I saw this bright pink blob from an upstairs window and thought I'd better come and investigate.' Tom lowered himself beside her. 'You sure this ground is dry enough? I don't want to add rheumatism to the rest of my troubles.'

'Your troubles?' chided Christie lightly. 'How can you say that when your troubles are almost over?' She leant back on her elbows and her glance was amused and affectionate, but dared not linger on the man sprawled full length beside her, getting grass stains on his white cotton trousers.

He'd taken off his shirt, infuriated by the problems of dressing comfortably with an arm in plaster. His tan was deep and smoothly olive. At his temples silver threads glinted in the sun.

That untamed lock flopped across his brow as he watched her from under heavy speculative eyelids. He was so attractive it seemed impossible to conceal her love for him a moment longer. But something held her back, for it was clear Tom hadn't joined her in her hiding place merely to exchange pleasantries.

He'd come there with a purpose.

She could perceive a question lurking in the black intensity of his gaze. Some query in his mind about her. She waited in discomfort: what would Tom demand of her now?

It took her by surprise, therefore, when he pushed out that arrogant bottom lip of his and countered, 'Almost over? If you only knew!'

If I only knew? . . .

Christie blinked uncertainly and tried to think straight in very difficult circumstances — alone with Tom Galvan, in this intimate place among the sweet-smelling grasses. It was an effort to be rational when all she wanted was to throw herself into his arms and hang the consequences. But what if he pushed her away in surprise and contempt because she too, without any intentional encouragement on his part, had succumbed to hero-worship? That would be impossible to bear.

Christie swallowed, with an effort, for her throat was suddenly dry as a desert. He could only be referring to affairs of the heart. Christie was to be his sympathetic ear and that was why he sought her out in this secretive spot. Thinking back, there hadn't been much communication with Diana Diamond over the past week — so far as Christie could tell.

'This place — ' Tom went on. 'What am I going to do with it? I can't afford the upkeep any longer.'

A note of weariness crept into his voice. 'Diana was right, the Manor will never be a family home again. It's a curiosity: a testimony to the enterprise of the medieval farmer. Though there's no other spot I'd rather live, I'm going to have to let the place go to auction. Perhaps an Arab will buy it, a pop singer, who knows?' He gave a bark of dispirited laughter.

'Bess and Stan have other plans: they're in their seventies and who can blame them? . . . Think of it, Christie, Galvans have lived here for over two hundred years. You know, my grand-mother spent almost half a million on the most painstakingly authentic restoration. You can see it in the way the old doors have been patchworked with new wood and fitted with copies of the original latches — Oh, she sold pictures, antiques, shares, everything but the kitchen sink to pay for it.'

'You never speak of your grandfather.'

'Perhaps that's because my brother and I never knew him. He was killed in Tunisia in 1943. Galvans have lived here for donkey's years.'

Tom rolled over and plucked a stem of sweet vernal grass, chewing on it reflectively. He gave an apologetic chuckle and touched Christie's cheek with the tufted end. 'Sorry to burden you with my troubles. I get maudlin on a day like this when everything's magic. France was good — but home is for real healing.'

'Tom — ' Christie hesitated, wondering if she was speaking out of turn, because after all, she was neither guest nor close friend.

'Mmm?' he prompted, eyeing the delicacy of her white shoulders and the roundness of her breasts beneath the taut cotton fabric. Her hair had been drawn back in a complicated sort of plait which swung down her back in a rope as thick as his fist. Her cheeks were pink — either from the reflection of her dress or from the warmth of the sun, he could not tell. When she spoke her thoughts he wasn't really listening, his mind full of his own plans — such as how to grab hold of her with one gammy arm. And would he get his face slapped?

'I know it's not my business,' said Christie tentatively, 'but as you say, the Manor *is* the perfect place to convalesce and I was suddenly struck by a thought. It seems selfish to want to save all this,' she gestured with a wide sweep of her arm, 'just for yourself.' He raised his eyebrows at her and pulled a face. 'Well,' she carried on bravely, 'I do think so.

'What if the Manor became a

convalescent home? You could still live here in your own quarters. But you've got another place near Joe's, haven't you? and you're more often there, I should think. Wouldn't it be marvellous to share this with people who've been very ill? Oh dear — '

Tom was listening now, frowning with consideration — though to Christie it looked like the beginnings of a storm over her impertinence. Nevertheless she was told to go on.

'You know the rapid turnover on the wards. It's not like even five years ago when patients were kept in for a second week of recovery. Because the beds are needed they're discharged home three or four days after quite major operations, and we all know this is far from ideal. We could send them to the Manor for a few days. And you — ' Christie was warming to her theme and determined to finish, ' — you and Dr Diamond could get married and live in the cottage! It looks quite large and if you did it up, built on a playroom — '

Tom's voice was a discouraging growl. 'Why are you so certain I'm going to marry Dr Diamond?'

Without any perceptible movement he had drawn ominously close, his eyes glittering down at her like steel.

To block him out Christie closed her own eyes and told herself to behave sensibly and not encourage trouble. But her elbows no longer seemed strong enough to support her and she sank back upon the grass. Why he should have said that, why he should imply he'd no intention of marrying Diana . . . why anything?

She quivered to find the dry warmth of his mouth gently testing her own response — a pair of questing lips apparently disembodied from the rest of him. Then the lips went away and she felt the beat of his breath on her hot cheeks, asking, 'And would you run this nursing home for me, dear Gertie?'

Christie didn't care even if she *was* reacting shamelessly. When impossible dreams were about to come true, it was no time for conversation . . . 'Anything you want!' she gasped, 'anything you want, Tom!' and fiercely her mouth reached for his and her arms and hands reached feverishly to pull the full weight of his body down upon her.

And if Bess's voice had not drifted out across the meadow calling, 'Telephone for you, Christie-e! Are you down there, m'dear?' Tom reckoned anything he wanted would have been his for the taking.

One brief interlude of unbridled passion had told him a great deal about the seemingly innocent Miss Wisdom, he brooded, pausing by the swimming pool and staring grimly into its murky depths.

Oh yes, Christie Wisdom's uncomplicated reaction to his experiment had confirmed his suspicions all right. He'd discovered exactly what he needed to be sure of.

10

'You sound rather strange!'

'Do I-er — darling? That's because I was a long way from the phone and had to run.'

'Hasn't Tom got one of those cordless efforts, then?'

'Well yes, James, he has, but I was down in the meadow — um — sun-bathing.'

'Very nice for some! *I*'ve just spent three hours in the post-mortem room and I'm frozen — it's like working inside a fridge. We've had a hepatitis case and all the technicians fled and left me to it. I assumed,' he went on, 'you would have some free time to see me.'

Christie shifted her bare feet uncomfortably on the chilly boards: she'd sped so fast across the meadow she had left her sandals behind. James sounded definitely aggrieved — and not without reason. She winced to recall the scene he had unwittingly interrupted. 'As I'd heard nothing I thought I should ring and check that the letters I sent on arrived safely. From both your mothers.'

It wasn't like James to be sarcastic. Sensing his crossness, Christie tried to summon up remorse for neglecting him, but her mind and senses were too absorbed with another to be capable of genuine feeling. He knew perfectly well that Olwen was more like an elder sister and far from being the wicked stepmother of legends. Besides, she was young and very beautiful.

'I got them — yes, thank you, darling.' She was trying now to sound soothing and placatory. 'Are you quite comfortable at the cottage? Your car starting okay in the mornings?'

'Yes,' came the terse response. 'Look, Christie, I'd very much like you to take an evening off as soon as possible. Something very important we can't discuss over the phone.'

Christie pondered this in stunned silence. Surely he couldn't mean that at last . . . An icy finger traced her spine. Absence, they claimed, made the heart grow fonder. But she had almost forgotten about James.

'It's a bit difficult,' she said desperately, playing for time. 'I'm here for such a short while. But I'll see what I can do. If it really is important.'

'It's important.' James sounded tense. He must be tired — overworking as usual, thought Christie, shivering with contrition as her passions cooled and chill reality stared her in the face.

'I'll ring tomorrow,' she promised, a sick ache gripping her heart. Such timing! James had finally reached a decision. And she knew she could never live with herself if she should hurt him deliberately. His voice came down the line rather sadly, 'Don't forget now. I'm missing you . . . '

Christie never cried. She forced back the bitter relief of tears. She had behaved badly out there in the meadow;

and now she must make reparation to James.

'I'll ring, darling. Missing you too,' she managed with an effort that made her hands shake as she replaced the receiver.

'Christie!' You couldn't choose who you fell in love with. But she had encouraged James to believe she loved him — indeed she'd believed it herself — and now she must live with the consequences.

'Christie?' repeated the low, questioning voice behind her.

She turned to find Tom listening — how long had he been there? — her sandals in his hand, a navy sweatshirt slung over his shoulders. 'You'll catch cold,' she said quietly, taking her shoes from him and avoiding his eyes. Adopting an attitude of dispassionate briskness that successfully disguised her misery, she tugged the sweatshirt over his rumpled head. Her voice was cool, forbidding further intimacy. 'Perhaps it would be as well to forgo the evening charts since we're going to Sir Frank's.'

'As you please.' Regret radiated from her since the boy-friend's brilliantly timed interruption. Fair play. Tom simply hadn't appreciated the seriousness of their relationship.

For the rest of the afternoon Christie neglected her duties and avoided Tom. He could have been risking his neck for all she knew, but she simply couldn't bear to be near him just now. He wasn't in his study and she suspected he had gone for one of his long walks to avoid her.

What on earth had possessed them? It could only be the heat.

* * *

Sir Frank Davy lived in a large Edwardian house in a leafy suburb on the posh side of the town. As they drove along the motorway Tom broke the silence to point out the spot where he had crashed. Christie began to feel sick.

She was no longer looking forward to the evening.

She had dressed to kill out of a sense of pride that the Wisdom head must be held high. And so with a steady, skilful hand a stranger had been created before her mirror, the fashionable and glamorous Christie Wisdom of old. Tom should not go out with a nurse tonight, but an exciting woman he could be proud of for a few brief hours. In spite of everything she wanted for one last time to read in his eyes the message that overwhelmed her in the meadow.

Christie studied her smooth waterfall of hair in the bathroom mirror. Pity it was so determinedly straight. But the colour was rich and shiny, and she'd learned all sorts of tricks to vary its style. With a comb as dark as her hair, she scooped one heavy tress above her left ear and dug the comb into place. Oh yes. Elegant and sophisticated, just right with the blue. And it made the most of her sparkling ear-rings.

'Well, you look jolly nice, Wisdom!'

she informed her image reassuringly. 'Nothing wrong in looking good once in a while. I don't know why I've been so hard on you in the past, throwing away your warpaint and putting you in all that dreary dark gear. They were right about the dress in Brown's. Azzedine Alaïa is a magician. The cut is extraordinary — those curves could be for real. And the colour is fabulous.'

Yet she had shrouded her transformation in a bulky reefer jacket and, nervily refusing Tom's suggestion of a drink in the drawing room before setting out, had driven Matilda up to the front of the Manor with a flourish, responding with a petulant, 'I know!' when instructed to turn left at the gates into the lane.

It was particularly disappointing that he'd made no comment on her Cinderella looks. He might not be able to see the whole thing, but surely he'd noticed she'd done something to her face and hair!

Must be in a mood, sulking, guessed

Christie ruefully. Well, goodness knows she deserved the cold shoulder after behaving so disgracefully. It wasn't as if he didn't know about James. Oh, what a mess her life had suddenly become — her carefully mapped out future turned into a jail sentence: and all because she'd been foolish enough to lose her heart to a man who had no need of it, but who had few qualms about taking advantage of any conveniently smitten female.

Christie was beginning to think she didn't much like Tom Galvan. Loving him, though: that was another matter.

He had not, apparently, noticed the sheer black stockings or, sniffed Christie, wallowing in gloom, the fact that she'd grown about six inches taller in the most divine pair of spindle-heeled ebony suede courts, reposing for the moment on the back seat as she drove in stockinged feet.

Tom got on to the subject of cars. He'd have to replace the Porsche.

Christie perked up a bit. She liked

cars, especially fast and expensive ones. Dad had changed his every five minutes, and she'd driven them all around town.

'What about the new 924S?' suggested Tom's chauffeur, and began to talk about digital fuel management systems and internally-ventilated disc brakes with such authority that Tom was once more staggered by the complicated Miss Wisdom. 'How the hell do you know so much about it?' he demanded, turning in his seat to examine his chauffeur's exquisite profile.

Just in time Christie remembered discretion. 'Look, is this where we turn off? Did you say Hamilton Avenue?'

★   ★   ★

Their hostess turned out to be none other than Sister Lewis, the Night Sister on Nazareth. Christie was at first astonished, then delighted to discover that Sir Frank had set the whole thing up to celebrate the couple's discreet engagement with a small party of close friends and neighbours.

'I'm so glad you've come,' whispered Marion Lewis as champagne corks popped and laughter flowed along with the Pol Roger. 'I find consultants en masse a bit intimidating. It's good to have another nurse here from Nazareth — though I must confess I didn't recognise you at first without your cap. Are you having an awful struggle taming our remarkable Tom?'

Christie just shook her head and smiled an enigmatic smile. She preferred the doctors any day to the self-important barrister from next door with his pompous manner and commanding voice. 'Marion, have I got a spot on my nose? Your neighbour keeps staring at me.'

'Everyone's staring at you. Especially your escort.'

Christie's hand flew involuntarily to her throat.

Marion caught Frank's eye and they

exchanged glances of satisfaction. 'Come and meet Perdita. I can see she's gloating over your dress.'

Perdita was the barrister's wife. She was also the owner of the snazziest boutique in the town, though mostly she did the buying and left running the shop to her minions. Perdita herself was in a black silk Bruce Oldfield number with a triple choker of pearls at her throat to disguise the fact that her neck was going. Her hair was styled in a chic blonde gleaming bob which she constantly tossed back like an elegant pony.

'Don't I know you from somewhere?' she drawled, signalling with her cigarette holder for more champagne.

'I don't think so,' replied Christie warily. It was most unlikely, after all this time.

'Perhaps I've seen you in the shop, then?'

'I doubt it,' murmured Christie with the faintest of smiles. 'I don't have occasion to dress up very often,' she added lest Perdita should be offended.

Tom suddenly materialised at her elbow brandishing a bottle of Pol Roger.

'Darling, you're so gorgeous and brown!' exclaimed Perdita extravagantly. 'Now do be careful — you've splashed champers on your DJ and I can see it's a silk mohair.' Her silver fingernail scratched at Tom's cream lapel. 'Now tell me, how was France, and how *are* you — truthfully? You promised you were going to introduce us to Diana Diamond some day. When are you going to bring her to dinner?'

'You'd better ask my nurse here for a health bulletin. Christie — ' But Christie had slipped away to help Marion in the kitchen.

Perdita's blue eyes glittered with curiosity. 'I could swear I've seen that girl before somewhere. You know, I'm sure I have. Now I wonder where it could have been? Never mind, it'll come to me — I've got an excellent memory for faces. But I simply can't believe she's a *nurse!* I mean to say, darling, she's wearing an Azzedine Alaïa.'

'A *what?*'

'He's a very upmarket designer, sweetie. Everyone's after his dresses. It's the seaming — makes a maypole look like Marilyn Monroe. No *nurse* could afford one of them. And you do realise those are genuine diamond drop ear-rings. What did you say her name was? Wisdom? Christie Wisdom?'

'You two sound like a couple of conspirators. What's going on?'

'Frank!' Perdita clutched his arm. 'Wisdom. Doesn't that ring any bells with you?'

'Ye-es, course it does. Archie Wisdom, the theatrical chappie. We were at university together. Sir Archie, I should say, but he's dead, as I recall.'

Perdita was getting quite carried away with her clever detective work. 'I knew I'd seen her somewhere before! That's his daughter, Christabel Wisdom. Used to be a *Vogue* model in the early eighties, then suddenly disappeared from the fashion scene. Rumour had it she got religion and went off to be a nun.'

Tom spluttered and choked and his eardrums fizzed. 'That won-derful jacket,' chided Perdita, slapping him on the back, 'do be careful. When are you going to get rid of this wretched plaster? It's ruining the shape to pin the sleeve up like that.'

'Don't say anything to her. Not tonight.'

Disappointment clouded Perdita's face.

'Perdita!' warned Frank. 'This is Marion's evening and I don't want it spoiled, look you. Christie's a nurse now and first-rate at her job. That's all that matters. She's made a new life for herself with us at Joe's. Convent indeed, my ****! I raise my glass to her, Tom — she's a grand little girl.'

Some little girl! mused Tom, appreciating his nurse's rear view swathed sexily in glorious blue, as she chatted with Brian Hastings, the cardiologist, and his homely wife. No wonder he'd thought her mysterious. She'd done quite a job in establishing a new identity for herself. The million-dollar question was . . . *why?*

'Christie thinks I should turn the Manor into a convalescent home for Joe's patients and extend the cottage for Diana and me,' announced Tom across the dinner table. Conversation immediately centred upon this innovative idea, but finally and with regret the consensus was that government cuts ruled the proposition out. 'Anyway, you'd never get Diana to leave London. Why should she give up her career to please you?'

'She will if she really loves him,' smiled Marion. 'I offered, didn't I, Frank? I said I'd give up night duty to look after you.'

'And I said you'd better not, we need the money!'

Under cover of the general laughter Brian Hastings leaned over to Tom and in a low voice said sympathetically, 'If you've a real problem there, Tom old chap, I might be able to help. Give me a ring over the weekend — if you're interested.'

As they drove home it was Christie who chatted more easily now; and Tom who was unusually silent. 'I think it's wonderful. Sister Lewis ... and Sir Frank Davy! None of us had the slightest idea! What a lovely evening, Tom. I must confess I thought I'd be out of my depth and that I'd only been invited out of politeness. But Marion seemed genuinely glad to have me there, and I did enjoy meeting the doctors and their wives informally. They all seem to be ex-nurses, don't they ... '

'Take the first turning on your left.'

Christie would have protested that to take the scenic route at this hour of the night was hardly advisable. But something in Tom's voice warned her not to argue. Perhaps he wanted to stop by the cottage and leave a note to tell Bess not to bother to come in too early as they would be sleeping late.

She flipped the headlights on to full beam, swinging Matilda round the tight corners, confident no vehicle would be venturing the other way. 'Pull in here!' rapped out Tom with an urgency that had Christie stamping on the brakes. 'Here, by the five-bar gate. And now,' he said, and his voice grated like ice, 'give me your car keys.'

A grim stranger loomed close by her side. Christie felt the stirrings of fear. 'What on — ?'

Before she could react he had leaned over and slid the keys from the ignition, tossed them in his palm, then closed his fist tight. 'Take as long as you wish, Cinderella Wisdom, but tell me all about it. I think I deserve an explanation. And we stay here till you finish.'

Her shoulders slumped. Her voice was a sigh. 'It was Perdita, wasn't it? She recognised me. Ah well . . . '

When she thought she had finished, Tom said, 'I have one question to ask you, and you may consider I have no right to your answer.'

Christie's fingers tightened over the steering wheel. But she was puzzled: for she felt sure Tom understood why she had sloughed off the old life as a snake sheds its skin. And she hadn't left anything out; she'd been completely honest with him, even revealing that she could, if she chose, lead the life of an idle rich woman.

The inherited wealth had seemed unimportant, something she generally chose to forget. She hadn't wanted her father's money; least of all as a result of his premature decease. Now the sudden realisation took her breath away — there could well be enough invested to keep the Manor from being sold!

'What?' Her thoughts had winged so fast and furious Tom's question went unheard.

'Did you ever,' he repeated bluntly, 'have a child?'

Christie pressed her fingers to her temples as if her head ached. She frowned in bewilderment. What . . . why should he . . . ?

'The boy beside your bed,' he prompted cruelly, his eyes lasering into the shocked face of his lovely companion. In the moonlight she seemed ethereal, a creature of the imagination rather than living flesh and blood.

Good heavens! Tom meant Ben. Tom thought Ben . . .

The hand clutching at his arm was warm and real enough. The soft laughter was music to his ears. 'That's my little brother. That is Ben,' she explained with warm and loving pride. 'Well, half-brother, to be accurate. When Dad died, Olwen was nearly four months pregnant. Ben's the best thing that ever happened to me and I love him more than anything else in the world. It's extraordinary: he's the image of my father.'

Tom felt drained with exhaustion and relief. He leaned across and turned on the ignition.

'Home, James,' he yawned — then wished he hadn't, because the effect on Christie was like a cold shower dampening her happiness. She looked as if the cares of the world weighed heavily upon her wide smooth brow. 'What's the matter?' he wanted to ask, but was sensitive enough to recognise that he had put her through sufficient interrogation for one night.

'No, don't drop me off here — drive round to the barn and we'll walk back together.'

He waited till Matilda was stabled and Christie came out of the dark interior of the barn carrying her jacket and shoes. Tom put his arm across her shoulders and in the moonlight as an owl hooted eerily from away over in the tall poplars he drew her unresistingly to him. She seemed so small and fragile now, so much in need of protection. What did Mallory suppose he was waiting for? If he didn't snap her up quick, someone else would come along and steal his woman away.

Careful now, Galvan, remember you're supposed to be a gentleman. Back off till you've got two good arms to show her how much you care.

He contented himself with a big-brotherly one-armed hug of the slim shoulders. 'You're beautiful tonight, Nurse Wisdom,' he murmured tenderly, 'but equally lovely in your uniform. I'm going to miss you when you're gone.'

There was a big lump blocking Christie's throat. She'd been sure he was going to kiss her again — and in this romantic setting she was in no mood to resist him. Especially when he reminded her of how short a time they had left together.

Mrs Capek had left lights on to guide their path. 'Would you like a nightcap?' asked Christie, eager to stave off the parting. 'Cocoa, perhaps?'

Before Tom could answer, the phone rang. Automatically his hand reached out, then drew back. He grinned. 'See how well trained I am? I thought for a moment I must be on call. What *is* the time? Gor-don Bennett!'

They both laughed, but the phone shrilled on insistently. He winced. 'Who the hell?'

'Cocoa?' whispered Christie as he put the receiver to his ear. From several feet away, she could hear a woman's voice — irritated because she had rung several times during the evening and got no reply whatsoever; urgent because of the importance of what she had to say.

'Cocoa?' she asked again, but Tom seemed to have forgotten she was there, so absorbed was he with his Diana back in town. 'Are you certain?' he was demanding. 'Tomorrow! — hell's bells, it's tomorrow today . . . Pleased? Pleased isn't the word for it. My *darling* Di — you know how frustrated I've been feeling.'

Christie slipped away and dejectedly her stockinged feet trod the winding stone steps to her room. Tom was dashing off to be with Diana first thing in the morning, and she'd need to wake early to drive him to the station.

Much more of this emotional torment she didn't think she could stand.

And there was James, wanting to have a serious talk about marriage . . .

* * *

But Christie was wrong about James.

She heard him out in silence with downcast eyes. 'Two years,' she said finally. He hadn't said a word about marriage. 'Two years is an awfully long time. A lot of things can happen in two years.'

They were sitting in a deserted corner of the staff dining room, James with a slice of mushroom quiche and a salad in front of him, Christie with a cup of lukewarm coffee. 'I didn't want to discuss it with you *here*,' he said irritably. 'Couldn't you have come over this evening?'

Tom had taken a taxi to the station. She wasn't even certain he'd gone to bed at all. She hadn't meant to eavesdrop — but plainly Diana had wangled some time off and organised a special licence so they could get married. This was Tom Galvan's wedding day.

There no longer seemed a reason to

put off seeing James. She'd gone to the hospital at lunchtime and dragged him from the path lab, knowing she must somehow find the strength to go through with it. He was grumpy at being disturbed and that made it even harder to summon up within herself the old affection. If only he could have pretended to be pleased to see her walk in out of the blue! Wasn't that how lovers were supposed to feel for each other? If Tom walked through those doors, now, her heart would turn over and the blood pulsate in her veins.

'I didn't know if I'd be free this evening,' she explained wearily. 'How long have you known about this, James? Why didn't you tell me there was a chance you'd be invited to join the research team at this American university?' And no suggestion, she reminded herself, that I should come too. Not a word of marriage. But oh yes, this is definitely a man's world. It would never do for the *woman* to initiate the proposal!

Motivated by feelings of pride and anger, she asked outright and boldly, 'Do you want us to get married, then, James? I know this isn't a leap year, but I assumed this was what our relationship would lead up to. No? I can see you don't. Fair enough. Do please eat your salad. No, I'm not heartbroken, I don't think we were ever in *love* with each other. But I hope we can still be good friends — and I do care enough to want to see you eating properly. Tell you what,' she urged, leaning across the table and squeezing his well-scrubbed hand. 'Before you go we'll have a vegetarian feast, how's about it, eh? When — when must you leave?'

James passed a hand across his face like a man spreading relief over his features. 'Next month. You will come out and visit me, Chris, in Boston?'

★   ★   ★

Christie was on the A27 doing seventy. She'd a holdall, already packed, in the boot and she'd left a note on Tom's study desk, though she didn't for a moment imagine he'd be back that day or night. Unless, of course, it was with Diana; and in that case Nurse Wisdom had no intention of playing gooseberry with a honeymoon couple.

Something in her bones warned that this job was over. She'd not be nursing Tom Galvan again. No one could complain if the nurse took a couple of days' leave.

Not wishing to turn up empty-handed as well as unannounced, Christie stopped for a while in Chichester and wandered round the shops in search of something special for little Ben. What a strange mistake Tom had made. He must have been into her bedroom to have seen that photograph.

She hunted out the perfect present for a diminutive fan: Paddington Bear in blue-and-white striped rugger shirt and boots, with a sweatband around his furry forehead — so comically appealing it brought a smile to her wistful face. She wished Tom could see it. She wished they were still together.

Then she was on the road again, yawning with a fatigue born of drained emotions and insufficient sleep. The traffic pulled in to give way to a speeding ambulance heading for St Richard's Hospital. Brief though the hold-up was, Christie felt her head begin to loll and her eyelids droop. She knew it would be more sensible to stop and rest, but some instinct forced her on.

At last she was safely there, turning into the curve of gravel drive fronting the flint and brick Chantry House, nestling in the lee of the South Downs. Ropes of wistaria with great purple swags of blossom fingered the bedroom windows, and species roses mingled with foxgloves and delphiniums in the borders. The front door stood open in welcome. Christie knew that she had been right to come.

She parked behind an unfamiliar BMW and was just dragging her grip from the back of the car when a slim blond man dressed in white came bounding urgently out of the front door. His face, she noticed in an instant of foreboding, was set and pale. Apparently he knew who she was.

'Thank God you're here at last! Olwen's been driven frantic trying to get hold of you. She's gone ahead in the ambulance. We're to follow in my car.'

Perceiving at a glance that Olwen's stepdaughter was on the verge of collapse, the man took control. He would explain while they were on the move. Meanwhile . . .

He slammed Matilda's tailgate and locked the passenger doors, raced back into the house and emerged, crashing the heavy front door behind him; tossed a dark blue seersucker jacket on to the back seat of the BMW along with Christie's things and hustled the dazed girl into the seat beside him.

As they roared out of the village and back on to the highway, travelling in the direction Christie had come from, she remembered the ambulance and knew. Tragedy was striking the Wisdom family yet again. And this time tragedy's victim was small, defenceless Ben.

11

'When they decided it was a brain tumour, immediately I thought of you, Mr Galvan. You're the most brilliant — Christie told us so much . . . she thinks so *highly* of you.' Olwen Wisdom's voice was broken with misery and fear, her face tear-stained, her huge blue eyes blazing with agony.

Her confidence dismayed him. 'I could do nothing for your husband,' Tom reminded her slowly.

'Ah, but you can save Ben. I know you can save Ben.'

'Mrs Wisdom,' he said gently, 'my business is neurosurgery. My task is to give my patients the best that is in me. I shall do my utmost to save your child.'

All the while he carried out the ritual preparatory scrub, Tom could hear Olwen's voice ringing within his head. She seemed hardly to have aged, was still outstandingly beautiful. Face to face with her once more, he had remembered that night at Covent Garden. 'Is there a doctor in the house?' had sounded the urgent call. He had been taken directly to their box, but it was too late to save the bearded middle-aged man felled by a massive and mortal coronary. There was a vague picture in his mind of a young girl crouching beside the body and clutching the dead hand: all Tom could recall was that she had shivered and trembled from shock.

As he rinsed and soaped and scrubbed again, Tom was unusually silent. Christie's little stepbrother . . .

With a vengeance Fate was plunging him back into the deep end of neuro-surgery.

'Patient's ready for you, Mr Galvan.' The nurses exchanged nervous glances. This was a different Tom Galvan, stern-faced and reflective. They preferred their confident amiable hero of old.

Dripping Hibiscrub, Tom yanked on

a pair of gloves and strode through the swing doors into theatre.

★   ★   ★

'But I don't understand! Why take Ben all that way to Joseph's, when Tom Galvan can't possibly operate?' Christie was wide awake now, nails digging into her palms as Mark Lawson revealed the gravity of Ben's condition. What could Olwen be thinking of, hiring a private ambulance and wasting precious hours when Ben's life hung in the balance? He should have gone straight to the Royal Sussex.

'You told Ollie he's one of the best brain surgeons in the country.'

'Not with one hand!' wailed Christie. 'Anyway, where do you fit into all this?' she demanded. 'And where is Ben's nanny?' If Olwen was beautiful but impractical, the Norland-trained Trudi had her head screwed on the right way. And she adored her little charge.

'With Olwen, of course. As for me,

I'm a first violin with the London Philharmonic and I'm living with Olwen during the Glyndebourne season. Any objection?' he challenged.

'It's nothing to do with me,' responded Christie wretchedly. That Mark was desperately worried about Ben was obvious from his pallor and tight-lipped profile.

'She won't thank me for telling you first, but we intend to marry in the autumn.'

A ghost of a smile flitted across his companion's taut features. Mark caught her eye and managed to respond. 'You have a snooze,' he suggested kindly. 'You look real whacked.'

★   ★   ★

The child lay face down in a sea of sterile green cloth, his shaved head clamped motionless, the surgeon peering intently into the wound in the back of the skull where the scarlet tumour had been.

Finally the tall masked figure straightened up with a great sigh of satisfaction. 'We've got it all!'

He glanced questioningly at Dr Guiles, the anaesthetist, who gave the thumbs up in indication that Ben's vital signs were strong.

Tom took a step back from the table. The only part of his face visible — the penetrating black eyes — said it all, ranging round the masked and gowned figures with an appreciation far beyond words. One neuro-surgeon back at the head of his surgical team: one more precious life saved.

'Brilliant stuff,' applauded Kingsley Armstrong. 'And the path. lab report shows no malignancy. We'll see how he responds in intensive care.'

Dr Guiles had taken charge now and was bending over the unconscious child on the operating table; Sister Calloway, the scrub Sister, was chivvying her wide-eyed nurses into action. The boss was back. And as ever, on top form.

Tom wanted to be the one to speak

to the child's family. To warn them that although Ben was not yet out of the wood, there was reason for cautious optimism.

Pulling off his mask, he left the operating theatre and went through to the dressing room to shower the sweat off his body. He knew that he had never performed better. And the pathology report had confirmed his intuition: high malignancy was not present within the tumour cells. Ben would be transferred to intensive care. The twenty-four hours following the trauma of surgery would be critical. What would happen to that space Tom had created when he cut the tumour out of the living brain? Now was the time for prayer.

Adrenalin still surged through his bloodstream and he felt reinvigorated, for the first time since his accident, filled with strength and power. But with a new sense of his own frailty, and a deeper compassion for the patients dependent upon on his surgical skills.

Under the shower he observed how

white his left arm was, compared to the rest of his body. In spite of all that physiotherapy and exercising, it was noticeably thinner than the left. But that was no problem: muscle tone would soon be restored.

The important thing was that the damaged hand and arm this day had functioned with the same old skill; had done their very best to heal Christie's little Ben.

★　★　★

'Shan't we be too early?' asked Christie doubtfully. 'The curtain doesn't go up till five-thirty.'

'Don't fuss, woman! I know what I'm doing.' Softening his forceful tone with a smiling sidelong glance, Tom took his hand from the steering wheel and gave her clasped fingers a reassuring squeeze. 'Come on now, it's not every night we get the chance to see your stunning stepmother in triumph on the Glyndebourne stage.'

On the short journey from Chantry House, where they were to spend the night, Tom had *twice* used the word 'gorgeous' to describe Olwen's voluptuous blonde looks. And now she was 'stunning', pouted Christie, who had pulled out all stops to catch her dragooned escort's fickle eye. The gentleman clearly preferred plump blondes (or bottle-auburn curls!) to dead-straight brunettes. And he was treating this venture not as a date so much as a do-good enterprise to rid his ex-nurse of her unfortunate phobia about opera in general.

'This is it. We've arrived.' The black and gleaming Lotus Excel nosed into the drive fronting the main house and swept round to the left and under an archway. The car park was a large field on a sloping hillside. 'Oh, lor'!' protested Christie, 'there's only half a dozen cars here. I told you we were too early.'

'All the better,' beamed Tom, 'to bag the prime picnic spot at the head of the lake.' He pulled up alongside an elderly Hillman estate, parked cheek by jowl with a gleaming new Rolls. 'Dear old Glyndebourne! Everyone's welcome and anything goes. The people who stick out like sore thumbs are the ones who don't give a fig about the music but boast that they've been here. You can spot the fakes a mile off.'

'I don't see that it matters,' said Christie argumentatively, 'so long as they can afford the price of the tickets. What's the marquee for? I didn't see that when I came with Dad's crowd. We dined in the Middle Wallop Hall. Salmon and strawberries . . . same as Olwen's packed for our picnic today.'

'There's candelit tables in there in case of rain. Grab a hold of this rug and I'll bring the rest. Bet you hardly recognise me with two good arms, eh, Gertie? I haven't seen you since you started your staff job on — which ward was it?' said Tom, pretending he didn't know. He had recently discovered the very interesting news that Dr Mallory had been brain-drained by the USA, leaving behind an apparently unconcerned Staff Nurse Wisdom.

'Gloucester Ward,' said Christie glumly. 'Men's medical. I'm very happy there.' Very happy indeed. It's so busy that I never have time to think of you, Mr Galvan. Pity they won't employ me twenty-four hours a day!

From somewhere in the rehearsal rooms came the sound of a soprano practising her scales. 'There's the stage door,' pointed out Tom. 'That's where Olwen told us to meet her afterwards.'

'There's hardly anyone about. Are you sure it's okay . . . '

But Tom was striding confidently ahead, disturbing the richly perfumed air of flower-filled gardens. Lovingly Christie's eyes caressed the dark curls on the nape of his strong neck, the breadth of his shoulders beneath the black cloth, the tapering waist and the shape of his toughly muscled legs.

Suddenly she found herself in a secret garden, a grassy glade at the head of the lake. 'Oh!' gasped Christie, wide-eyed, for it was the most decidedly romantic spot that Tom had chosen. 'Now we dump all this stuff right by the water, dash back in the dinner interval at about seven o'clock, fish up the champers and have ourselves a feast.'

Christie tilted her head to one side and her fingers played with the silk rose pinned to her pink satin choker. Tom was fastening a length of string round the neck of a champagne bottle and lowering it into the lake to keep cool.

'Don't go falling in, Tom,' she warned.

'Darling girl, it's not at all deep. Not here at the edges anyway.' He grinned at her concern, and shook his head, then held out his hand to her and drew her to his side. 'Come along, you ravishing creature.' He slipped his arm about a tiny waist made even more impressive by the fullness of the rose taffeta skirts and the strapless bodice which seemed to defy gravity.

'It's not yet three.' Her eyes had a wild dazed look as he gazed down into their depths, the pupils large and black.

'So long,' he murmured, 'since we've been alone together. We must make the most of today.'

She was wearing her hair in the mermaid style Tom liked best: with a side parting, a silken waterfall that fell over one eye à la Jerry Hall, spilling way below her shoulderblades. There was a white silk rose pinned at her waist and another on her white silk purse. To Tom she was not Christie Wisdom, RGN, but a fairytale princess.

He grew suddenly impatient. His change of mood was disturbing after the blatant admiration she had seen in his eyes. Christie bit her lip, sure that something about her was wrong, not pleasing to him.

'Come on. While we have the lake to ourselves let's make the most of it.' He pulled her arm around his own waist, underneath his jacket so that she could feel the warm hard muscles of his back. Her heart began to thunder against the tight pink bodice. She couldn't trust her voice, so she kept silent and tried to match her steps to his. No man should be aware how much he was adored. It wouldn't be good for him. The rolling South Downs and the herd of grazing cattle beyond the ha-ha, the waterlilies and the dragonflies — she saw none of them. Her world held only Tom.

Their dawdling steps got slower and slower. Tom couldn't hold out even to the halfway point. When he drew her into his arms and rained passionate kisses on her eyes and throat and naked shoulders there was no question that he loved her or that she loved him. At last he drew apart and said, 'Dearest Gertie, I've got something for you,' delving into his pockets and coming up with a small red jeweller's box.

Christie's heart went into a gallop. Only in her wildest dreams had she pictured such a scene.

When she saw the delicate ear-rings nestling in a shell of white satin, she could have wept with disappointment — but, well schooled in hiding her

344

emotions, she lifted trembling fingers to fix the pearls in her ears, sensing this was what Tom expected her to do. 'A special thank you to my special nurse — Gertie.'

Feebly she protested there should be no extra reward for just doing one's job. But Tom laid a finger on her struggling lips and delved into his pocket again, this time coming up with a royal blue box which he opened himself, then reached to capture her left hand.

'Diamonds are forever — isn't that right? — my mysterious love, my angel in disguise?'

It wasn't a proposal in the old-fashioned way, but then the predictable would never be Tom Galvan's style, her man of action, her one and only love. And he wasn't giving her the chance to refuse.

★　★　★

Not until the dinner interval could Christie begin to think rationally again.

But she was okay. No tension, no phobias. Tom could feel her body, pliant and totally relaxed, lolling intimately against his as they drank champagne from the same glass. They had finished their strawberries and cream and heedless of their finery sat huddled together by the lake, sharing Tom's jacket as the evening grew perceptibly chillier and the dusk fell.

Christie couldn't hold back a hiccuping giggle. 'Didn't Ollie look — er — stunning in that enor-mous black wig?'

'What a voice! Not a big part, Frasquita, but she certainly made an impact. Fine figure of a woman, your stepmother. Of course, a bit of weight helps a singer. I must say,' he added, 'it's refreshing to hear an opera sung in English instead of Italian or German. All right for the privileged few with Swiss mothers living in the German-speaking area of Zurich.'

'Tom — Careful now, that's your bad arm.'

'What bad arm? I'll have you know I'm in perfect shape — and don't you snigger!'

Christie snuggled closer, holding out her hand and admiring her engagement ring in the deepening twilight. 'Dear Tom, I wasn't! Remember that late-night phone call you had from Diana? I thought you'd dashed off to get married by special licence. I'd no idea she'd booked you in for this new medical electronics test at the Royal Hanoverian. I still don't understand how it works, how they could tell your fracture was well healed.'

'I'm none too clear about it myself. Suffice to say it involves the use of pulsed electro-magnetic fields to detect the pace of healing in fractured human bones. *Comprende?*'

'Ben owes his life to Diana. If she hadn't hustled you into being tested, you could never have carried out emergency surgery on him. Shh! Let me finish. I must know, Tom, if she's going to be terribly hurt about our engagement, because if she is . . . '

Her lover stopped her protests most effectively, until the interval bell summoned them back into the opera house. 'Diana made her choice. And I was the loser, or so it seemed at the time. I fell in love with you the very first time I saw you, when I knew nothing about you.' Arms entwined, they joined the sauntering throng of ladies in long summery gowns and their formally dressed escorts. Tom began to list all the things about Christie he hadn't been aware of at first sight. 'That you were Archie Wisdom's daughter. That I'd ever seen you before. That you were once a real live *Vogue* model. That you were anything beside a trained St Joseph's nurse. All these things you were, my angel in disguise.'

Christie pulled a face. 'You've missed out the rich woman bit. Do you realise if we pool our resources we can probably keep the Manor going?'

'Ah,' said Tom, subsiding into the

plush seat beside her in the small and surprisingly unsumptuous auditorium. 'I may have found a compromise. Have you ever heard of the Heritage Trust? They buy and renovate historic buildings, then let them out all year round to anyone interested in holidaying in a Heritage.'

They stood up to let a party of five get to the middle of the row. 'Go on,' urged Christie, 'how does that help you?'

'Well, I've had someone round to look at the place and they're interested in taking over the medieval wing and dividing it into two flats, while we keep sole use of our end of the Manor. Use it as our own holiday home and perhaps have a family house in the town. What do you think?'

Christie was gazing up at him, her face so radiant with adoration that Tom quite forgot the drama of *Carmen* unfolding before them.

'I think you're wonderful, Tom Galvan. That's what I think.'

'Shhh!' chided a music-lover in the row behind. 'For goodness' sake!' And the lovers in the row in front winked at each other and smiled.

THE END

We do hope that you have enjoyed reading this large print book.

Did you know that all of our titles are available for purchase?

We publish a wide range of high quality large print books including:
Romances, Mysteries, Classics
General Fiction
Non Fiction and Westerns

Special interest titles available in large print are:
The Little Oxford Dictionary
Music Book, Song Book
Hymn Book, Service Book

Also available from us courtesy of Oxford University Press:
Young Readers' Dictionary
(large print edition)
Young Readers' Thesaurus
(large print edition)

For further information or a free brochure, please contact us at:
Ulverscroft Large Print Books Ltd.,
The Green, Bradgate Road, Anstey,
Leicester, LE7 7FU, England.
Tel: (00 44) 0116 236 4325
Fax: (00 44) 0116 234 0205

ACCIDENT PRONE

Anna Ramsay

From hospital ward sister to sanatorium sister at Ditchingham Prep School is a drastic change, but Ruth Silke needs something different. Working with Dr Daniel Gather, the local GP who covers the school, isn't so easy — particularly when he seems all too matter-of-fact about his young son Danny, a boarder at the school. Ruth is convinced that Danny's accidents are a cry for help, but how to persuade Dan? Particularly when their own relationship leaves so much to be desired . . .

FAIR FLOWER OF NORTHUMBERLAND

Harriet Smith

Amanda believes that Justin is cold-bloodedly planning to marry her step-sister for her money. She allows him only one good quality: he is clever, especially at putting her in the wrong. When she is forced to revise her opinion, she admits that she judged too hastily — but the last thing she expected was to find herself fathoms deep in love with the object of her distrust . . .